Sugar MINE Summer

KAY MAREE

Contents

This is a work of fiction. Similarities to real people, places, or events are entirely coincidental.

SUGAR, MINE

First edition. January 2018

Copyright © 2018 Kay Maree.

Written by Kay Maree.

Cover Design © Designed With Grace - http://www.designedwgrace.com/
Cover Images © Adobe Stock & Deposit Photos
Editing – Susan Horsnell & Word Writer Pro

Social Links

Facebook:
https://www.facebook.com/kay.maree.334
Twitter:
https://twitter.com/MisKay85
Goodreads:
https://www.goodreads.com/book/show/34528910-angel-mine?ac=1&from_search=true
Goodreads Author Page:
https://www.goodreads.com/user/show/65394903-kay-maree

About the Author

I live in Newcastle, on the New South Wales coast of Australia with my husband and three beautiful children.

Between being a taxi for my children, and working full-time, I somehow find the time to write. It's something I love with a passion and with the encouragement of my very supportive husband, I have accomplished one of my dreams – releasing my first novel.

I hope you fall in love with my characters as much as I have.

I love reading and getting lost in a good book when I manage to snatch five minutes to myself.

Kay Maree

Dedication

I dedicate this to all my Sugars out there.
May all your dreams come true. xx

I also dedicate this to my beautiful friend Kirstymarie. You are an amazing person and you deserve nothing but happiness. You wanted Sergio's story and I just hope I did him justice. xx

Prologue

Laying back on the hard ground, patchy with grass, I wriggle to get comfortable. I gaze up at the darkened sky, the moon full, the stars bursting to life. I squeeze my eyes shut, wishing for the millionth time for things to be different and wondering why I can't have a normal life. I search my memory, trying to remember the life I once had with my parents. A sharp pain squeezes my heart and I rub my chest. I'm reminded of the fact, they threw me away and pushed me into hell to repay my father's debt. Words run on an endless loop from that night when I was ripped from my bed.....

"Judy, we have to let her go to pay him back." My father's voice boomed and echoed around me as a strange woman dragged me from my parents' house. "It's her or us"

They were the last words I heard from my father before he turned his back on me and walked away. I

Shaking from the memory of my dredged-up thoughts, tears pooling in my eyes, I turn away from the night sky. A lonely dandelion sways in the gentle breeze. Picking it, I sit up and cross my legs. Closing my eyes again, I picture myself as a happy child laying in a field of beautiful dandelion puffs and making silly little wishes. Lifting the white puff to my mouth, I let out a soft breath and on a whisper, send out a wish. A wish so simple, but for me, out of reach. I watch as dandelion puffs float around me, hoping that one day, my impossible wish could come true

I cringe when I hear the screen door slam open, it hits the wooden banister on the back porch with a bang and flinch at the sudden sound of Karen's raspy voice breaking through the quiet of the night. "You silly, stupid bitch."

I turn and in the glow of the moon, I see the rage I know so well distorting her face. I have no doubt about what comes next. I used to be terrified, would shake out of control at the sight of her rage, but in time I learned not to show fear. She thrives on fear and it made everything so much worse. Now I remain detached, show nothing, feel nothing except for the little bit I allow myself when I sneak out and lay amongst the dandelions and stare at the stars.

Scurrying to my feet, I straighten my nightgown as it falls to my knees. Wrapping my arms around my waist, I bow my head allowing my dark hair to drape around me like a veil. I cross the patchy lawn and slowly pad up the stairs.

Before one foot lands on the hard wooden porch, Karen reaches out and grabs my arm, dragging me the rest of the way. Her nails bite into my skin, but still I show her no sign of pain.

"You stupid bitch, how dare you be outside without my permission. You know what's coming now, don't you?" She shakes my arm, piercing the skin as she drags me through the house toward my room.

Room, hah, fucking prison is more like it. There are no happy memories in this house, this room only heartbreak and torture.

As she swings the door to my prison cell open, I glance at the dirty mattress lying on the floor. Still I feel nothing. She throws me to the ground and I know what's expected. Without her having to say a word, I kneel and rest back on my heels, remove my nightie, place my hands on my bare legs and dig my nails into my thighs. I hear a cupboard door squeak open, close my eyes and suck in a breath when I hear the unmistakable sound of a belt snapping together. Once I would cower in a corner on hearing that sound, but over the years, I have learned to accept what follows.

Slowing my breathing, I feel the air around me shift as the first sting crosses my back. Then, another and another, I have no idea how many follow. I've become used to the pain and clear my mind of thought, my body of feeling until I hear the belt being placed back in the cupboard.

"After all these years I would have thought you'd have learned by now, stupid bitch!" Karen rages.

I nod my head in response, not trusting my voice to speak.

She crosses the room; the door slams and locks click into place. I release the breath I was holding and bend forward, placing my hands on the dirty carpet in front of me. Cool air stings the wounds on my back and the metallic smell of blood surrounds me. Taking a few deep breaths, I slowly crawl to the mattress. Lying face down, I let the tears flow and my small wish of a new life seems even further away.

As days pass, my arms reach for the impossible, but I continue to hope there is someone out there who can free me. I stare through the small dirty, cracked window until sleep finally takes me.

Chapter One

Seven years later...

Kirsty

The click of high heels sounded on the tiled floor outside my door, startling me from a restless sleep. I push myself up to sit on the thin, worn mattress on the hard metal cot where I'm forced to sleep these days. I lean my back against the cold concrete wall, sending a chill through my body. I hear the clink of locks being unbolted and pull the thin, torn sheet around me. The door swings open and hits the wall with a bang causing me to jump.

"Time to get up," Karen snarls. She stands in the doorway, blocking my view of the hallway.

I nod, wrap the sheet around me tighter and slowly get to my feet.

11

"Drop the fucking sheet."

I grip the sheet, my protection, tighter in my hands. But, one glance at the opposite wall where metal chains and cuffs are attached, reminds me – fighting Karen will result in me being strung up again. I release my grip and the sheet floats soundlessly to the cement floor, settling at my bare feet. Looking down, I note the ratty brown singlet and black undies I'm wearing. Placing my hands behind my back, I run my fingertips over the welts lining my wrist. They are from when I first arrived at my prison and I was attached to the wall, chained and handcuffed. I'm not sure how long I was kept there as I faded in and out. Memories of Karen's men entering the room, forcing water down my throat and touching me in places which made my blood run cold, flood my mind. I squeeze my eyes shut, not wanting to think about what they might have done had Karen not walked in. When she saw them fingering me, she blamed me for teasing them. The beating I received caused me to believe it was the end. Now, I wish it had been.

I'm snapped back to the present when Karen speaks again. "Time to see the boss."

My stomach twists as images of his previous visits flash through my mind. I bite my lip to stop the sob which wants to escape and try to relax my face into a blank expression. I guess I don't pull it off quick enough because Karen's maniacal cackle of laughter adds to the fear pulsing through my body. I'm terrified of what's likely to happen.

Bowing my head forward so my hair covers my face, I make my way to the door

"Head up you little, bitch. You should feel grateful he's kept you around for this long." Karen yanks at my arm; her nails piercing my skin and shoves me into the long hallway. I squint my eyes, trying to adjust to the bright light as she pushes me forward to the stairs leading up to the main house. I can't remember the last time I was permitted outside to see the sunshine, the moon and the stars.

I guess ending up here in this new prison is my own fault. Although Karen beat me, warned me, I couldn't fight the urge to sneak out and lay under the stars. The previous places had fortress like fences surrounding the properties so it's not as if I could have escaped. Shuffling my feet, I painfully climb the stairs while she continues spitting words at me.

"I'm not sure why the boss insists on keeping you around, why the fuck he's kept you for so long, you're nothing special. You're nothing but a mousy little girl who insists on disobeying. You never learn. Your life means nothing, *you* are nothing"

***

Stopping in front of two large wooden doors, I suck in a breath and allow the feeling of nothingness wash through me. A feeling I'm used to. I flinch when I hear a male voice roaring from the other side of the door. Pushing me roughly to the side, Karen steps forward and pushes the doors wide open. Lifting my head, I stare into the eyes of a monster. A monster who has kept me captive for almost ten years.

"Ah, my little piece of pie." I try not to cringe at the sound of his booming voice.

He waves his arm toward me, ordering me to enter. My feet drag, reluctant to take me towards the pudgy, balding man who controls my life in the palm of his hand.

"Head up girl," he demands.

Not one to be argued with, I snap my head up at the sharp edge to his voice.

The doors close behind me with a thud, but I don't dare take my eyes from the man standing in front of me. I step closer as he insists, he runs his hand down the side of my face and further, until he reaches my breast. He squeezes hard and I try desperately not to wince at the pain and the stinging feeling in my chest from the bite marks he left last time. But, he sees through me and a sadistic smirk curls his lips. His eyes dance with laughter knowing the pain he is causing me.

"I see you're still sensitive from the last time we saw each other." He chuckles and releases me, pushing me forcefully to my knees. "Today my dear, you're going on a little trip." He pats my head before strutting around me.

I nod, mistake, he was looking for a verbal answer. He grips a fistful of hair and yanks my head back hard; my scalp burns from the force. I answer, "yes, sir." It's then I notice the other two men in the room.

"That's better." He releases me and pats my head again.

I try to sneak a look at the other men, but my focus is drawn back to Bruno J. I'm not allowed to call him by name, I'm not even supposed to know it. But, being someone's prisoner for so long, it's not hard to overhear who he is.

"Bruno." The man to my left speaks with a raspy voice, as if he smokes a packet of cigarettes a day.

I zone out as they speak, not really giving a shit what they have to say. My mind is filled with the fact, I'm going on a trip. I wonder if there might be a way for me to escape and finally be free. I'm drawn back to the conversation when Bruno yanks me to my feet and slams his mouth down on mine. I struggle to stop myself from gagging at the foul stench of his breath.

"Little pie, I'll see you soon," Bruno promises.

His hand darts between my legs and he grips me hard. Before I can react, I'm pushed toward one of the men, he catches me in his arms before I hit the floor.

Bruno laughs. "Enjoy my whore, gentlemen."

My heartbeat pounds in my ears as he leaves the room, I'm now at the mercy of these two strangers. I should have listened to the conversation between the men instead of daydreaming about escaping and being able to live a normal life. I have no idea what is in store for me.

"Okay, little pie." One man says as he grips my hair and wrenches my head back. "Time to find out what all the fuss is about."

I swallow past the lump in my throat, wondering what he means. The other man twists my arms behind my back and secures them with something which digs into the welts at my wrist. I wince and tears prick my eyes.

"Joey take this little slice of pie back to the compound, I need to speak to Bruno about something else before I join you."

"Yes, sir," the man called Joey says. He pulls me back into his chest and I feel the hard ridge of his cock digging into my ass. As the other man leaves the room, I feel Joey's hot breath on my neck "Time to go, whore," he breathes into my ear making my skin crawl.

Chapter Two

Sergio

Pulling the car into an empty car space in front of Silverwater jail, I blow out a deep breath. I'm gearing myself up to face Antonio. I know he's pissed with me and I wouldn't blame him if he comes out and punches me in the face for losing his girl. I squeeze my hands around the steering wheel, my knuckles turn white and I feel the twinge of pain in my wrist from the car accident, another time I let down the boss. I'm amazed I'm still breathing. I feel the tension in my shoulders and know I could go a few rounds with someone right now. I roll my shoulders and shake off the feeling.

There aren't a lot of people in this world who can intimidate me, but Dominic and Antonio – they're the kind of men you don't fuck with and when you are part of their family, you follow fucking orders. Failure usually means death in our family, but I have been given a reprieve so, I have a lot to prove right fucking now.

The leather creaks under the strength of my grip and I release the wheel. I drag my fingers through my hair before stepping from the car and flipping my shades down to block out the blinding sun. I hold my hands up before me and study the tattoos before running my fingers over the cross with the Italian flag draped around it. Marcella's name is inked below the cross and there's a nine-digit number I will never forget. I rub my chest, feeling winded all of a sudden and read the words cicatrici è uguale a forza (scars equal strength) on the top of my other hand. I'm torn from my thoughts when my cell phone rings. I retrieve it from my pocket and don't bother checking the caller's number, I already know who it is. "Boss"

"Si Sergio, Antonio released yet?"

"No, still waiting."

"Si, we may have a lead at an old warehouse on the outskirts of Sydney. The minute Antonio is released, you both head straight there." He pauses for a moment. "Sergio, I want fucking answers, no fucking excuses."

"Si, Boss." There's an edge to his voice and I know what he fucking intends if I don't get the information for him. He rattles off an address, I'm lucky I have a good memory. "On it, Boss."

"Bene, call with any news."

"Si." I click 'end call' and return the phone to my jacket pocket. I hope to fuck this lead gives us something positive I can take back to Dominic. I look up at the sound of someone approaching and catch sight of Antonio heading towards me. As he moves closer, I lift my chin and reach out my hand.

"Capo Bastone."

"Si, brother, it's good to see you."

I'm surprised by his greeting and wonder if he actually means it as I shake his hand. I can tell he's pissed by the slight edge in his voice. We climb into the car but before I can say anything he beats me to it.

"So, do we know anything new?"

"Boss rang while I was waiting for you to come out, he said we may have a lead at an old warehouse not far from here."

"In Sydney?"

I nod my head, equally confused as to why Katherine would be in Sydney. "I don't fucking know Capo Bastone, but we are going to find out. There's a present for you in the glovebox."

Leaning forward, Antonio opens the glovebox and removes his Colt super 38's, I watch as he weighs them in his hands before slipping them into the back waistband of his pants. I lean back in my seat and feel the comforting outline of my own guns pushing into my back, I relax a little more in my seat.

"Well let's get this shit over and done with. I want my woman back, and God help the figlia di madre (motherfucker) who has her. They're going to wish they'd never been born once I'm finished with them."

Starting the car, we fall silent as I weave my way through traffic and head towards the address Dominic gave me.

"Sergio, where's your phone?"

Grabbing my phone from my jacket pocket, I hand it over to Antonio. "Who are you calling?"

"Theo, things aren't adding up, it feels like we're missing something."

"Si." I nod in understanding because like I said, I don't get why Katherine would be in Sydney. I focus back on the busy road and the next thing I know, Antonio has disconnected the call and hands it back to me.

"Sergio, we need to get there now. Fuck, the tracker on her phone is on and if it moves, Theo will let us know."

I hear the urgency in Antonio's voice, nod and press my foot down on the accelerator. I hope to fuck we're not too late.

Chapter Three

Kirsty

I shuffle through the front door, Joey pressing behind me and pause at the top of the steps to breathe in the fresh air. It feels like forever since I've felt the warm sun on my skin. Closing my eyes, I lift my head and soak in as much as I can until I'm jolted forward by a hand pushing against the centre of my back. I stumble but quickly catch myself before I hit the ground.

"Move it bitch, we don't have all day."

I take the steps down cautiously. When we reach the bottom, Joey grips my arm and steers me towards an old rusty white van. Sliding the door open, he pushes me inside with so much force, I have to roll onto my shoulder so my head doesn't hit the other side of the car. Righting myself, I look around and realise there are no seats except for the long bench seat in front. The windows back here are all covered over, I can't see out and no-one can see in.

"Hands."

I whip my head back towards Joey when he speaks, he remains standing at the opening of the door, watching me. I scan him from head to toe. He's dressed in dirty clothes and it doesn't look like he's had a shave for at least a week. I turn around and while Joey cuts the restraints free, I look down and realise I'm still in only my singlet and undies. He spins me around and pulls a pair of handcuffs from his back pocket. My body trembles as visions flash past my eyes of the last time I was bundled into a vehicle and handcuffed.

He attaches the first one and I suck in a breath when it clicks into place. He reaches into the van and loops the free end over a bar on the ceiling of the van. Raising my other hand, he clicks the other cuff into place. I close my eyes and take deep breaths to calm my racing heart and shaking body. They snap open again when I feel Joey's hot breath skim the side of my face.

"I wonder if you taste as good as you look."

I jerk my face away and the minute I do, I know it's a mistake, confirmed by the stinging slap across my face. Gripping my chin, he forces my face back to his and his lips crash down on mine.

He clucks his tongue at me after he pulls back and licks his lips on a hum. "So, you still have some fight in you, that's good."

I study his eyes, for the first time I notice how dilated they are and the sheen of sweat across his forehead.

"Good to know, little pie. You and me are gonna have fun." He chuckles as he shimmies back out of the van and slides the door closed with a loud bang.

I look up at my cuffed hands and don't even attempt to try and escape, I know there's no point. Resting on my ass, I try to get comfortable. I don't bother to take notice when I hear the car door opening and slamming or when the engine starts up. I keep repeating to myself, I just have to get through this drive until we reach my new prison. Dropping my head, I let my hair fall around me and stare down at my lap.

***

"What's your name, little pie?" Joey's voice breaks through the silence surrounding us, he asks question after question about where I grew up, how old I am. But, I don't answer. I keep my head down, peeking through my hair at the rearview mirror, watching as his eyes dart from the mirror to the road ahead. I drop my head again, there's no point telling him anything about me or who I am, *I* don't even know who I am anymore. The girl I once was has disappeared, little by little, day by day, with everything that has happened over the years. The car jerks violently and the force causes my head to slam against the side of the van. I try to bite down on the yelp, but it escapes my lips anyway.

"That got your fucking attention," Joey sneers.

I wince with the pain exploding through my head and feel the van driving on rough gravel before coming to a sudden stop. He hits the brakes with such force, I'm thrown back and my arms are stretched painfully. I'm still dazed when I hear the door slide open, I try to clear my fuzzy brain.

"So, you don't want to fucking talk to me you, little bitch? Well, that's fine, I have ways of making you talk."

After unlocking the cuffs, he drags me from the van by my hair and throws me to the ground. I grunt when my knees are pierced by the small rocks on the gravel driveway. I look around and notice the old warehouse the van is parked next to. Is this my new prison? A sharp pain erupts across my stomach when Joey kicks me and I roll over and hit the ground. He laughs as tears flood my face and I wrap my arms around my stomach.

"Get up." He spits at the ground beside me.

When I don't move, he reaches down and grips my hair so tight I swear some of it is pulled out by the roots. Somehow, I manage to scramble to my feet. The rocks dig into my bare feet.

"When I say get the fuck up, I mean, get the fuck up." He releases my hair and wraps an arm around my throat. I instinctively grip his arm to take some of the pressure off my throat, I can't breathe.

"Don't worry little one, you and me are going to have some fun before I take you to the compound," he breathes into my ear before he drags me toward the warehouse.

****

I'm pushed into a dark room at the back of the warehouse. It looks like an old office which hasn't been used for a long time, it's covered in dust. Joey shoves me into a corner, I slide down the wall and bring my knees up to my chest, wrapping my arms around them I pull my legs in closer.

I watch as he paces the room and drags his fingers through his hair until he comes to a sudden stop and stares at me for a moment, as if in a trance. He seems to snap out of whatever trance he was in and starts picking up old papers strewn on the ground. He crosses to the other side of the room where there's an old fireplace in the wall. Pulling a lighter from his pocket he sets the paper alight and throws it in.

Joey has his back to me, he seems mesmerized by the flames. I glance toward the door and wonder if I can sneak out while he remains transfixed. I shuffle on my bum, closer to the door, watching Joey to make sure he's still not looking my way. I look back to the door and slide closer, but I freeze in my tracks when I hear the unmistakable sound of a belt snapping together. My attention returns to Joey, he has a belt in one hand and what looks like a metal rod in the other.

"Where do you think you're going, bitch?"

"Nowhere," I whisper

"Crawl to me."

As I move towards him on my hands and knees, my eyes dart between the belt and the metal rod.

"Kiss my shoes," he spits out.

Not what I was expecting, but bending forward I take a deep breath and blow it out, before my lips touch the top of his shoes. I scrunch up my nose at the stench of him.

"What a good, little bitch."

I cringe as I see his hand with the belt lift, it comes down across my back and I close my eyes against the pain. He hits with much more force than Karen. His laughter echoes around us. I dig deep and push the searing pain to the back of my mind as he pushes me to my back with his foot. Crouching beside me, he pulls down the strap of my singlet, exposing one of my breasts. He licks his lips as he grabs me and squeezes.

"Looks like your *Sir* has marked you already."

I turn my head away as he cups my breast and runs his fingers over one of the bite marks still visible from Bruno J.

"I think I need to add to your collection."

I feel his hot breath against my skin, making it crawl. I brace myself for the pain from his teeth, but when I feel nothing, I wonder if he's changed his mind. I open my eyes to see his arm stretched out, the tip of the metal rod glows red then white in the fire. Abject terror squeezes my stomach and for the first time in a long time, I can't control my mouth.

"No. no. no!" I cry out when I realise what he's going to do.

"Enough, you be a good girl and stay still."

I try to push away, but he anchors his knee into my stomach, pinning me to the ground. He lowers the bar towards me and I'm helpless. The metal rod grazes my arm, burning the tender flesh before he holds it to my breast. Pain like I've never felt before shoots through me. My head spins and I let out a scream as tears stream down my face. When he removes his knee, I scramble to the wall. The room is spinning, my head is pounding, chest throbbing with pain. I have no hope of getting to my feet. He steps in front of me with the belt in his hand. I cower and whimper, knowing I probably won't make it out of here alive. My time has finally run out.

"Now for that taste." He raises his arm with the belt and I wait for the impact.

A loud bang echoes around us as a door is slammed open. Joey spins around as two other men enter the room with guns raised. I push myself into a ball against the wall, I feel dizzy and sick. Then a man speaks and I raise my eyes to stare into deep midnight eyes swimming in worry.

"It's okay, I won't hurt you." His voice is husky and he has a thick accent which I can't quite place at that moment. He offers his hand to me, but I stare at it, not sure what I should do. I look towards Joey, but he isn't looking at me anymore. He's occupied with staring down the barrel of a gun.

"Signora, I won't hurt you, you're safe now."

I glance at his hand again before looking back into his eyes. I see kindness and something deep inside me urges me to trust this stranger. Stretching out a shaky hand, I place it in his. The touch sets off a live wire inside me and I jump. *What the fuck is going on?* I feel confused, but shake it off and allow this man to pull me to my feet and into his chest. On shaky legs and gripping his jacket in my hands, I push the pain I am feeling to the side and inhale his intoxicating scent. He seems to awaken something deep inside me, something I thought died a long time ago.

Hope.

Chapter Four

Sergio

"Sergio, get Kat out of here while I tie up this figlia di mandre." Antonio manhandles Joey towards him. "The Boss has been looking for you..."

I ignore the rest of what Antonio is saying and make my way over to the terrified girl cowering against the wall, I can tell straight away it's not Katherine. Crouching down in front of her, I move slowly so as not to scare her anymore then she already is. Her glazed eyes are darting everywhere. I need her to concentrate on me. I need her blinded from what's happening around us and focus on me.

"It's ok, I won't hurt you."

Holding out my hand, I speak softly and hold back the anger I feel on seeing the horrific injuries scattered across her body. I want to kill the figlia di madre (motherfucker) who has caused the fresh burn marks to her arm and breast. I suck in a deep breath and release it slowly to calm myself then turn my focus back to her big brown eyes. They are full of sheer terror and my heart twists in my chest, I need her to know I won't hurt her.

"Signora, I won't hurt you, you're safe now."

Her eyes glance at my outstretched hand before gazing back into my eyes, hopefully she sees the truth in my words. I feel elated when she starts to place her shaking hand into mine, she feels some measure of trust. As our hands connect, I feel an electric shock jolt through my body. Such a simple touch causes us both to jump and our eyes lock, I know she felt it too. I calm myself with a deep breath, now isn't the time to be wondering what the fuck it was.

She stands and I draw her to my chest, holding her close. She is shaking uncontrollably, probably shock from her injuries. All I want to do is sweep her into my arms and carry her out of here, keep her safe. But, my first priority is to back up my Capo Bastone.

A deafening noise pierces the air and I snap away from my thoughts. It's the familiar sound of a gunshot, I hold tesoro mio tighter in my arms and run my hands up and down her back to soothe her. She stiffens at my hold and I ease off to look down at her. I'm worried I may have hurt her.

"Did I hurt you?"

She shakes her head and I see the sadness in her eyes.

Joey's screams pull me back to what's happening around us, Antonio is losing control. I need to tell him the woman isn't Katherine.

"Capo Bastone! It's not Miss Katherine!" My shout is more of a roar to get above Joey's screams.

Antonio snaps his eyes my way and looks at the girl in my arms, it takes everything in me not to cover her up. I feel her grip me a bit harder and her shaking intensifies under Antonio's gaze as he slowly moves towards us. He stands in front of her so she doesn't have to look at the piece of shit on the floor. Leaning forward, he places his hand gently on her shoulder. My protectiveness kicks in, I don't want Antonio to touch her. When I feel her push closer into me and relax slightly, my possessiveness eases a little with the knowledge she's chasing my touch.

"Can you tell me if a redheaded woman was here?"

She shakes her head and her body trembles. Shock, cold, I feel like an absolute cazzo for not covering her up sooner. Slipping off my coat, I wrap it around her shoulders and pull her closer, not wanting a centimeter between us.

I look at Antonio and he nods his head, he understands I'm not letting her go. Our attention is drawn back to the girl in my arms when she speaks. I lean closer to hear her soft, raspy voice.

"No one e-e-else w-was here," she sobs.

"Fuck!" Antonio growls and pulls at his hair.

The girl flinches in my arms and huddles closer at the angry edge to Antonio's voice.

"I promise we won't hurt you, what's your name?" Antonio asks gently.

"K-kirsty."

"How old are you Kirsty?"

"Twenty-five." Her voice is a little stronger now and she glances between Antonio and me.

I lock eyes with Antonio, thinking we may be able to get some answers now her body has stopped shaking and her voice is a bit stronger. I have known this man for many years and I can see in his eyes, he's thinking the same thing as me. I nod so he understands we are on the same page.

I bend my knees and stare into Kirsty's eyes. For a moment I'm lost, I don't see so much fear anymore.

"Tesoro mio, I need you to tell me what happened. How did you get here?"

Kirsty starts to speak but slams her mouth shut when Joey screams out. She cowers against me.

"She won't tell you shit if she knows what's good for her."

I'm about to lose my shit when Antonio gets my attention.

"Sergio, we need to get her to the house. Take her in the car with you and get Doc to meet you at the house. I'm gonna tie this piece of shit up and throw him in the van. I'll take him to the docks, get Dom to meet me there."

I nod my head, but I'm not fucking pleased with his idea at all. I need to have his back. Kirsty's sobs break through my anger and I realize, Antonio is right, I need to take care of her. Wrapping my arms around her tighter, I lower my lips to her ear.

"It's ok Sugar, I've got you."

She nods against my chest. I give Antonio a chin lift and lead her from the room. Sobs rack her tiny body as she is overcome with pain. She leans against me heavily, I'm not sure she can walk much further.

I bend and whisper in her ear, worried if I pick her up without saying something first, she may freak out.

"I'm going to pick you up, okay?"

"O -o-okay," she sobs.

Bending my knees, I sweep her into my arms and hold her close against my chest. She relaxes slightly and burrows into me.

"T -t-thank y -you"

"Always, Tesoro mio." Fuck, why do I keep calling her that? I don't even know this girl, but the minute she gripped onto me, it was like our fate was sealed and she became mine as much as I became hers.

Chapter Five

Kirsty

I'm not sure why I told strangers who I was. Something told me I was safe with them. The closer the man called Sergio, held me, the more relaxed I felt. His touch surrounded me like a protective cloud, it was the safest and most comfortable I have ever felt. Words flowed, I couldn't and didn't want to, stop them.

One look at Sergio and I should have been terrified, he should have scared the shit out of me. He's big, muscular and towers over me. Every visible piece of skin is decorated with tattoos, his hair is dark, close cropped. He is an ominous figure. But then, I gazed into his eyes and the gentle caring within, took my breath away.

I wanted them to know who I was and was willing to tell them everything. Until Joey broke into my thoughts with his screaming at me. Shouting out, *if I knew what was best for me, I would keep my mouth shut.* A timely reminder that I know better than to open my mouth about anything.

I tried to be strong and not show these men any fear, but I was scared. What if these men only said I was safe to gain my trust. I don't know who they are, what if Bruno J or even Karen sent them here to test me? I don't know what to think anymore, I'm so confused.

When Sergio held me, wrapped his coat around me, I couldn't stop my body's reaction to him. I knew I could trust him from that moment on. If Bruno J had sent them, why was the guy called Antonio asking if another girl was with me? He would have known, but if Bruno J didn't send them, how did they know where we were?

I'm pulled from my thoughts when Sergio stops in front of an expensive looking black car. I shift my weight, readying to stand and pain explodes through me. I can't prevent the whimper and groan which escapes my lips.

"I've got you, Sugar, relax."

Sergio's hot breath wafts over my ear, but instead of making my skin crawl, I feel heat creep up my neck. I turn my face into his hard chest so he doesn't see the obvious redness. His heart is thumping hard and fast under my cheek and I feel him suck in a deep breath. It does something to me that I can't explain. Again, I wonder what the fuck is happening to me? At the first touch of kindness and it's like my body just decides to surrender itself to this man who I don't even know.

He shifts my weight in his arms and I prepare for him to put me down. Instead, he shifts me into one arm while he opens the car door with the other.

"You can put me down to make it easier." I speak quietly.

He shakes his head and gently lowers me into the backseat of the car. I moan as pain grips me and when I look up, his eyes are fixed on me. His eyes are troubled, like he has an internal war with himself happening. After a moment, he appears to shake it off and then closes the door.

I feel an overwhelming loss, being out of his arms. I have to fight the connection, there is no point trying to get close to this man, or any man for that matter. He may be nice now, but if experience has taught me anything, it's that feelings can change as quickly as they emerge.

You would think, after all these years, the thought of any man saving me would have become non-existent. I can't help but think this man is different and a feeling of hope washes through me. I should push it away, but I don't want to, I want to grip it with both hands and savor it.

I'm so lost in my thoughts, I hadn't realized Sergio had climbed into the car until I hear the engine tick over. The radio comes to life and the radio announcer's voice makes me jump. It's been forever since I've heard any type of music.

"We are at number five on our all-time favorite songs countdown," the man says before announcing the next song - *Hero* by *Enrique Iglesias.*

The first bars of the song play through the speakers, I glance into the rearview mirror and connect with eyes as dark as night which hold so much emotion. I try to relax into the soft black leather seats, but no matter which way I move, pain shoots through me. I take a few deep breaths, hoping it eases.

"I'll turn it off if you want," Sergio offers. "The radio I mean."

I shake my head before finding my voice. "No p-please leave it on"

He nods, keeping his eyes on me for a moment more before switching his gaze back to the road. I feel the loss of contact shoot through me and think, maybe it would have been best if he'd turned off the radio because as I listen to the words, I have all these crazy thoughts racing through my head telling me, maybe he could be my hero. Tears prick my eyes and I gaze out the window as the first one escapes. I quickly wipe it away so I don't look weak and desperate for any kind of connection.

I wrap Sergio's coat tighter around me, his calming scent surrounds me. Leaning my head against the window, I watch as cars zoom past. I rub my hand, remembering the jolt I'd felt when he first touched me and wonder if he felt it too. I attempt to focus on the scenery as we pass instead of the silly thoughts filling my head.

I'm not sure how long we've been on the road, my head is fuzzy and I feel nauseous. I jump at the sound of Sergio's voice and it takes me a moment to realize, he's on the phone. I don't want to seem rude, but I can't help overhearing part of the conversation. The words in English, that is. I try to pinpoint the other language he's speaking, but I'm becoming more and more lightheaded, the pain much worse. I wonder if now that the adrenaline is wearing off, I may be going into shock. It's a feeling which isn't unfamiliar, actually it's quite common. Sergio's voice sounds strange in the background, it's like I'm in a tunnel and no matter what I do, I can't quite bring myself out of it.

"Boss... I'm on my way back... Call Doc... Joey figlia di madre... Antonio ... Si Boss, be there soon."

I glance up at the mirror again and see the worry in his midnight eyes. My head droops and a chill breaks out across my body causing me to shake uncontrollably. I welcome the feeling, because anything is better than the pain racing through me.

"Kirsty, stay with me, Sugar."

Sugar, such a special name for someone you care about. So, why does he insist on calling me, Sugar? I'm nothing special. Like I've been told thousands of times, I'm nothing, never have been and never will be. My head is spinning, my chest is thumping and I close my eyes needing to stop everything from moving so fast. It's no use, everything continues to spin behind my closed eyelids. I hear his deep husky voice, full of concern, but I can't respond.

"Tesoro mio, come on stay..." The last words I hear before everything goes black and those midnight eyes follow me under.

Chapter Six

Sergio

"Tesoro mio, come on stay with me"

I watch as her head drops and know her body has gone into shock, I've seen it enough times in my life to know. I swerve to the side of the road, shove the car in park, jump out and grab a blanket from the trunk. Racing around to her side, I rip the door open and catch her before she falls out onto the ground. Laying her down on the seat, I wrap the blanket around her and rub her shoulders to warm her up before placing my fingers to the pulse point in her neck. A soft whimper escapes her lips.

"I'm sorry, Sugar."

At least she's still breathing and her pulse is weak, but regular. I blow out the breath I've been holding since I stopped the car and glance at the watch on my wrist. It's another half an hour before I can reach Dominic's home where Doc will be waiting. I need to get her home now!

She's so tiny, so badly injured. I hope to fucking Christ I can get her to the house in time. I check she's secure, slam the door shut and jump in behind the wheel. I can't wait to get my fucking hands on Joey, the piece of shit, I want answers for my precious tesoro. Once Kirsty is settled with Miss Brooklyn, Dominic and I can and pay the cazzo a visit

***

Pulling into the long drive leading up to Dominic's house, I feel my body tense, kick into gear like it does before a fight. I know Kirsty is still breathing, I've heard the soft whimpers she's been making, but I need Doc to see her right now.

Not bothering to park the car in the usual place, I stop by the front door, switch off the engine, jump out and jog to the passenger door. Nobody, and I mean *nobody*, is going to be carrying Kirsty but me.

"Sugar?" I breath into her ear before easing from the car and holding her up close to my chest. I get no response. Taking the front steps two at a time, I don't get a chance to open the door. Brooklyn is standing in the door way, wide eyed and staring at Kirsty in my arms. I shake my head to indicate things are bad.

"Can you take Evie, she can't see Kirsty like this." Kirsty is wrapped in a blanket but part of her upper body is exposed, both it and her face are a mess.

"Doc   is   upstairs."   Brooklyn   understands immediately, turns and hurries into the lounge area the best she can with the cane she needs to use because of her fucking piece of shit ex. She calls out to Dominic.

"Big man, I need to take Evie to Gwen's, while you help Sergio."

"Si, Angel." I'm surprised to hear Dominic speak, as I take the foyer stairs to the top floor, I'd assumed he'd be on his way to the docks to join Antonio. I meet up with Doc coming out of one of the spare rooms.

"Sergio, in here." He indicates the room he's just come from.

Nodding, I stride past him and note he has the room set up and ready. I take Kirsty to the bed and lay her down gently. I pause for a moment, not ready to let her go. Until I feel a hand on my shoulder.

"Doc you need to..."

"I know." He pauses, seeming to weigh his words. "Dominic needs to speak with you, I'll tend her. You know I'll do my best."

I nod, but I'm reluctant to move. What if this is the last time I see her?

"Sergio." I hear Dominic's deep voice from behind me and look towards him, he's in the doorway staring at Kirsty. He turns his eyes towards me and nods.

"Doc," I growl low. "If she dies you're gonna wish you'd never been born."

With my threat hanging in the air between us, I watch as Doc's eyes widen and he swallows before nodding.

Grunting, satisfied he seems to get it, I take one last look at my girl before moving towards the bedroom door where Dominic is waiting.

"Fuck," I growl. When the fuck did I start thinking of her as my girl. I shake my head, not giving two shits if it's too soon after meeting her. I knew she was mine the moment our hands touched. The sharp jolt to my insides was like nothing I've ever felt before.

***

"What the fuck happened, what didn't you say over the phone?" Dominic demands to know as we step out into the hallway.

"We went to the warehouse as planned, but Katherine wasn't there." I blow out a breath as everything hits me all over again. The blood curdling scream, Joey standing over Kirsty with a belt as she cowered against the wall like a scared animal. "Joey was there and he was torturing the poor girl."

"Fuck," he growls, dragging fingers through his hair. "Do we know who she is?"

I shake my head. "Not really. The only thing she managed to tell us is, her name is Kirsty and she is 25 years old before Joey yelled at her to shut her mouth if she knew what was good for her."

"Where's Joey now?"

"Antonio is taking him to the docks as I said on the phone, he wants you to meet him there."

Nodding, he paces the floor before coming to a stop and staring at me. "Do you think Kirsty is still in danger?"

"Si, I believe so, Boss."

"We'll see what the fuck the Doc says about how bad her injuries are and go from there. I'll head to the docks and meet Antonio. I'll call Demetri and the rest of the men to meet us there."

"Boss, I want to be there."

He stares at me for a moment then, looks to the now closed bedroom door where Kirsty is. "She means something to you." It was a statement rather than a question.

"She's mine," I growl before I can stop myself.

Studying my eyes, he must see something there and nods in understanding. "This is going to be a long path for you, are you sure you want to go down it again?"

I don't even hesitate with my answer and it kind of pisses me off that he would even ask. "Fuck, Boss. I fucking felt it."

"Watch it, Sergio," he growls back before squeezing my shoulder.

I nod, not trusting myself to speak. I have never spoken to the boss like that before. His eyes soften a little as he glances towards the stairs leading down to the front door when we hear it close.

"Si brother, I get it." Is all he says before stepping over to open the bedroom door.

***

Following behind Dominic, we re-enter the room and I see Doc wrapping a bandage around Kirsty's arm where earlier I'd noticed fresh burns. A sheet was draped over the rest of her body, she looked so small in the big bed and all I wanted to do, was hold her.

"Doc?" Dominic's voice draws my attention back to the Doc.

The man finishes bandaging Kirsty's arm and turns to face us. "This girl has been through so much, I'm surprised she isn't dead. I had to remove the coat and her singlet before I could see the full extent of her wounds."

"You fucking what?" I squeeze my hands into fists at my sides to stop myself from punching him in the face. How dare he see my girl naked!

"Enough, Sergio." Dominic snapped.

I breathe deeply to control the anger coursing through me as Doc continues speaking.

"As I was saying. I had to remove her singlet so I could assess her injuries. I have applied cream to the wounds on her chest, as well as the burn to her breast, she was covered in bite marks and bruises. *Human* bite marks. The bruises will fade over time as will most of the bite marks, but some were quite deep lacerations and I would expect them to leave scars."

I suck in a deep breath as everything the man is saying hits me square in the chest. I glanced down at my hand which reads cicatrici pari forza (scars equal strength) and I hope to fuck it's also true for Kirsty.

"I found numerous old scars which appeared to form a pattern across her body. Some scarring is quite old. When I rolled her over to examine her back, I found numerous fresh welts as well as older, faded scars. Some asshole has been lashing this girl's back for a very long time."

"Fucken shit," Dominic growls in anger.

I'm barely holding myself together right now. "Doc will she be ok?"

"At the moment..." his head cocks toward the tiny figure in the bed. "....as you can see, I have I.V. fluids containing antibiotics on run through. Once this bag is done,

I'll set another to run through over twenty-four hours. I've given her a strong sedative so she'll rest and give the shock time to settle. If there are no complications, she should wake in about four to six hours. She'll be tired and in extreme pain when she does wake up so, make sure you have some painkillers handy for her. She's to have plenty of fluids, water preferably and if she wants to eat, keep it light. Try and encourage her to eat, it will aid her recovery. She's very malnourished so four or five small meals a day would be ideal.

"Is Brooklyn coming back?" I ask Dominic, not wanting Kirsty to be alone while we take care of Joey.

"Si, she wanted to drop Evie off and come back to see if you needed anything. You know how she is, she's a natural born mother."

Nodding, I cross the room and take a seat in an armchair in the corner, needing to be near her until Brooklyn returns.

"Doc, can we talk outside for a moment?" Dominic asks before leaving the room.

I bend forward and rest my head in my hands, praying my girl wakes up. After everything the Doc has told us, I can't wait to find the cazzo who has done this and make him pay for every second of pain he has caused her. It was obvious her life had been harsh, but I saw a glimmer of her strength when Antonio was talking to her in the warehouse. I hope to fuck she can keep fighting and stay with me.

Chapter Seven

Kirsty

I bite my lip and hold back the scream which wants to escape. If I don't, it will fuel her need for cruelty, her need to make me suffer for longer. So, I squeeze my eyes shut and allow the tears to stream down my face. I swallow the metallic taste of blood from my lip. I pull on my arms a little, but it's no use, I'm cuffed and chained to the wall, ensuring there is no escape from the onslaught.

"You little bitch, are you really stupid enough to think you can escape?" Karen whips my back again, increasing the force and causing the strands to bite into my back.

I rest my head against the cool concrete wall hoping for it to be over soon. I wasn't trying to escape, I only wanted to be out in the fresh air, to see the moon and the stars.

I snap back to the present when I feel the heat of Karen's body pressed up against mine. I flinch when my back begins to sting with the pressure. She licks up the side of my face and the overpowering scent of her perfume surrounds me.

"I love the taste of your tears, knowing I've caused them. Remember, there is no escape from here, from us. We would always find you." Her cackle is maniacal as she steps back and continues my punishment.

***

Springing forward, I clutch the silken sheet to my chest. My entire body is trembling, sweat pours from my face, mingled with tears. I'm still half-trapped in my nightmare and I scramble back until my back hits something hard. I become more alert and darting my eyes around the semi dark room, I notice light coming from a small lamp on a table beside me. Confusion causes my heart to beat hard, I wait for my eyes to adjust to the dim light and look around. This is a beautiful bedroom, I finger the soft sheet, softness I've never felt before. *Where the fuck am I?*

The door knob rattles and I begin to panic. Pushing my back against the hardness, the sheet slides through and I notice I'm wearing only my undies. I grab at the material and wrap it tighter around me. It's then I see the drip in my hand and when I glance up, a bag of fluid overhead. I brace myself, eyes fixed to the door, waiting for someone to enter and steeling myself for whatever may happen.

"Hello, you're awake." The voice is soft, kind and I watch as the beautiful blonde approaches the bed. In her hands are a bottle of water and a sandwich in plastic wrap. She places them on the bedside table and speaks again. Her voice has a reassuring warmth to it.

"I'm sorry if I startled you and I'm sorry the sandwich is wrapped instead of on a plate. It's difficult for me to carry a plate safely and use this at the same time." She indicates the cane in her hand which is supporting her.

"It's okay," I whisper. I'm not ready to relax despite the kindness of this woman, it could be some kind of trick.

"Do you mind if I sit?" She indicates the bed.

I shake my head and watch as she slowly lowers herself. "My leg hurts if I put weight on it for too long."

I nod in understanding and wonder if I can ask her where I am.

"Would you like a drink? Doc said you need lots of fluids." She reached over, grabbed the bottle of water and unscrewed the lid before passing it to me.

I hold out a shaking hand, accept the bottle and take a sip. Closing my eyes, I revel in the sensation of the cool liquid sliding down my parched throat. It alerted me to just how thirsty I was and I gulp a few more mouthfuls. I groan with satisfaction and hear a soft laugh. I feel my face heat with embarrassment, bow my head and let my hair fall around me.

"I'm sorry, I didn't mean to upset you. Doc said you'd be thirsty and I was thinking, maybe I should have brought up an extra bottle. Then, I pictured myself trying to carry said extra bottle up the stairs. It was quite a challenge to carry what I did." She laughs again, at herself and her struggles.

I can't help but laugh with her at the image she has placed in my head. I can't remember the last time I laughed and something inside me twists at the realization. I start to relax, convinced this beautiful, kind woman means me no harm.

"Um, can you tell me where I am? What happened?" Her soft eyes stare at me and I notice a flash of sadness cross her face.

"You're in my home. My name is Brooklyn. Sergio and Antonio found you and Sergio brought you here to Newcastle. My fiancé, Dominic, along with Sergio, left to...." She pauses for a moment seeming to weigh her words before going on. "....meet up with Antonio to settle an issue, but trust me when I say you're safe now. No-one can hurt you here."

She reaches for my hand and I automatically cower from her touch. The moment she sees my reaction, she pulls back. I feel bad about the way I reacted.

"I'm s-sorry," I sob.

"I understand, but please trust me. I promise you no-one will hurt you while you're here."

Nodding, I wipe my face with the sheet and place the bottle down on the bedside table. "Why don't I have any clothes on?"

"Doc removed them so he could treat your wounds."

The sheet has slipped slightly, revealing the white bandages around my chest. I give Brooklyn a questioning glance."

"Doc said you'll be in quite a bit of pain for a while, you have a lot of injuries. He's left painkillers and antibiotics to prevent infection."

I lower my eyes, take a moment and lift them to hers as I speak. "I couldn't say no to what was happening. I had no choice, she would have killed me." My words tumble out and I finish on a sob. "I'm not weak."

"It is obvious, you aren't weak. Doc said you have been tortured for a very long time." She sounds sad and I see it in her eyes.

She eases closer to me, I remain still, tense. She reaches out and pats my leg before sliding nearer. "I'm just going to give you a hug," she whispers.

I nod in understanding, she wraps her arms around me and smooths her hand lightly over my back.

"I'm sorry this happened to you and I promise you, Sergio and Dominic won't rest until they find out what happened to you, why it happened, and deal with the people involved."

"I don't want anyone to get hurt." I ease back from her hold.

"You have to learn to trust us. I know it will be hard but I'll be here whenever you're ready to talk."

I want to open up to this woman but I'm afraid. How can I trust? The last time I did, I was taken from my bed and used to repay a debt. Brooklyn seems to sense, I'm not ready to open up.

She pats my hand. "Have something to eat and get more rest. I'll be back later with some clothes and when Sergio returns, he'll explain more." Brooklyn pauses and her eyes look deep into mine. "Sergio won't rest until he finds out everything about you. I saw it in his eyes when he carried you in, he'll only rest when he's killed whoever did this."

"Th-thank you." Images of the morning flash past my eyes and I take a few deep breaths to relax. "you're safe" plays on a loop in my mind.

I think about what Brooklyn has said and again wonder if I can trust these people or is it all a trick. Will Karen be here to take me back the next time I open my eyes? Tears roll down my cheeks and my stomach clenches at the thought. I roll over, place a pillow under my chest for support and take the sandwich from the side table. As I unwrap the plastic, I feel Brooklyn stand and then the soft click of the door closing. I wait for the clink of locks being slid into place, but it doesn't come.

Brooklyn seemed so sincere, can I trust her. With all my heart, I want to. I bite into the sandwich and ponder what will happen when Sergio returns. I wonder if Joey is the issue which needed to be settled.

My hands shake as I bring the sandwich back to my mouth for another bite. No use worrying, I'm too weak to go anywhere right now, too weak to fight, so I'll make the most of their kindness and see what happens next.

Chapter Eight

Sergio

Leaving Kirsty at Dominic's place was so fucking hard, but knowing she's there with Brooklyn made it a little easier. Even though Dominic said I didn't have to go to the docks with him, I had to. I have to get answers from that piece of shit for her before I kill him.

As I drive towards the docks, the Boss in the passenger seat, I can feel the anger rolling off him in waves. His hands are clenching his thighs. He's itching to get his hands on Joey too, it wasn't long ago he tried to run us off the road with Brooklyn and Evie in the car. What made the incident worse, was Dominic had just found out Brooklyn was pregnant. Anyone taking on the Boss when he's alone is a fucking idiot, but taking him on with his family present is a death sentence. Joey's death won't be quick, it will be long and painful. He should have prayed he'd never be caught.

I draw the car up to the old warehouse which runs along the back of the docks. After switching off the motor, I jump out and jog to the passenger side to open the door for Dominic. Images of Kirsty cowering in the corner of the filthy room where we found her run through my head on an endless loop. I can't help wondering, after hearing about her old injuries from Doc, if what she was suffering was more of the same for her. Was it just another day in hell for my girl? Pure rage bubbles through me when I think of what she's been through. I want to get this shit over with, make sure Joey suffers and get back to her.

"Sergio, I know you want answers for your girl, but you need to remember, Katherine is still missing. We need answers, *she* is our priority." Dom rests his hand on my shoulder and I nod. "I promise, we will get the answers you need even if it means we'll be here all afternoon."

"Si, Boss." I'm distracted as Demetri's car comes to a stop next to mine. Johnny, Nico and Demetri jump out and stride toward us. Not in the mood to talk about this shit any longer, I turn towards the door ready to get the answers all of us fucking need. I slam the door open with force and the sound echoes in the night. We all head to where Antonio will be waiting and as I glance at the other men, I think it's apt that we look like a death squad.

"Looks like the party is about to begin, Joey boy." Antonio taunts before laughing.

We round the corner to where they are and find Joey tied into a chair. He spits out, "Fuck you" to Antonio. Bad move. Antonio swings and his punch shatters Joey's jaw. He yells out in pain.

"I want him on the table," Dominic orders. He steps around me and points to an old wooden table in the center of the room.

"Si, Boss," Demetri acknowledges. He and Nico step forward, cut the ropes holding Joey and drag him toward the table.

Joey is obviously not one to give up. He starts spewing shit at us and fighting to get free. "You guys are already dead and you don't even know it yet."

"Shut the fuck up," Nico growls

"You may as well just kill me now."

"That would be too easy for scum like you," Demetri says as he ties him to the table.

"Sergio," Antonio pulls my attention away.

I stride to where Antonio is standing beside another table where knives are lined up.

"How is Kirsty"

"I don't know. She passed out in shock before I could get her to Doc. When the Boss and I left, she still hadn't woken up. Doc cleaned her up, started a drip and now we just have to wait and see. Brooklyn is with her."

I don't tell him about the marks which scar her entire tiny body. They're not hard to miss, but now isn't the time to discuss what Doc said about previous beatings and injuries. I don't yet know what happened, why she was there, to give him any answers yet.

Antonio glances over my shoulder and I realize he's received a signal from Dom when he waves his hand over the knives, inviting me to select one.

I pick up a skinning knife and weigh it in my hand, it will do nicely. As I step toward the table, Joey starts chuckling. It grates down my spine, this piece of shit is still so fucking cocky even though he's the one strapped to a table in his underwear, like a fucking animal. Bringing the knife up to the light, I watch as the beams bounce off the curved blade.

"Am I fucking amusing you, you traditore?" I spit out.

His eyes bounce back and forth between the knife and me. I watch as a sheen of sweat breaks out over his forehead.

"So, are you are going to tell me what I want to know?" His eyes are locked on mine, but he doesn't say shit. I twist and play with the knife in my hand. I'm not use to having one, my fists are usually enough, but with this fucker, he deserves everything that's coming to him.

Running the tip of the knife down his chest, I watch him suck in a deep breath as the knife slices into his skin and blood pools around the blade.

"Who gave you the girl?"

"I found the whore on the side of the road," he hisses out.

Three quick slashes across his chest and I ask again once he finishes screaming out.

"Who gave you the girl?"

"Bruno J," he wheezes out after catching his breath. "Gave her to Billy, who gave her to me to take back to our compound."

"Why?" When he doesn't answer, Demetri jams a cloth in his mouth to shut out his screams and I slice him a few more times.

He nods that he's ready to answer and Demetri removes the cloth. His eyes are wild and blood covers his torso. "To pay a drug debt he owed my boss."

Dominic steps closer to the table. "What the fuck did he just say?" Rage radiates off him.

"Fucking trash," Antonio snarls.

"Who's your *new boss?*" I demand to know. Fucking cazzo is so fucking high most of the time he has no loyalty to anybody, let alone his family.

"Fuck you!"

"Fuck me? No, fuck you, traditore."

Stepping over to the 'instrument' table I drop the knife, pick up a pair of pliers and cross back to the table. Joey has been in these situations often enough to know what's coming next and squirms, pulling against his restraints. I smile at his reaction.

"Who is your fucking *boss*?" I demand to know while I place the pliers on one of his toes and apply pressure before twisting.

"Paulie DeMarko," he screams out as I hear the crack of bone.

The name registers in my head and the pliers slip from my hand, echoing as they hit the concrete floor.

"Fuck!" Dominic shouts. He paces the floor, dragging fingers through his hair.

The other men glance at us both, confusion written all over their faces.

"Boss, please. I need to get to Kirsty now. I need to move her."

He nods. "Go. Now. You know where to take her.

"Si, Boss."

I don't need to be told twice. I jog from the warehouse, jump in my car and the tires squeal as I floor it away from the docks. I have only one thought in mind, I need to get to Kirsty and I need to get to her right now.

Chapter Nine

Kirsty

"Time to meet the boss," the woman I have come to know as Karen, says.

I stand, feeling the dirty carpet beneath my bare feet. I step towards her, but she holds up her hand for me to stop.

"He'll be here in a minute, get down on your knees."

Lowering to my knees, I try to control the trembling wracking my body. It's been the same for the past two days since I arrived, it doesn't seem to want to stop. How do I know it's been two days? I've watched the sun rise and set through the tiny window of my new room. I grip the bottom of my nightgown nervously. A raspy, booming voice from the doorway captures my attention immediately.

"Ah, there's my new little pie." I glance up to see him rubbing his hands together as he steps closer. His voice sends chills down my spine and I close my eyes, hoping for the millionth time since I arrived that this is only a nightmare and I'll wake up soon.

"Eyes up!"

Snapping my head up, I study the man in front of me. Balding head, pudgy, short man who looks about fifty years old.

"Little pie, get to your feet. I want to see what I own now."

I want to fight him and tell him to fuck off, but when I did that to Karen last night, it didn't end well for me. So, I climb to my feet and try to bring the trembling under control.

"That's better, now I can get a good look at you." He reaches out to touch my face and shrink away from him. His nose flares and I whimper when he grips my hair and yanks my head back, forcing me to look at his face.

"I own you, remember that," he growls into my face and his foul breath wafts over me.

I struggle not to throw up as I nod. I'm revolted when his hand pushes up my nightgown and whimper as he cups me between the legs.

He releases me and orders, "strip." He steps back giving me room to remove the nightgown. With hands shaking uncontrollably, I grip the bottom of the gown and slowly start to lift it over my head.

"Hurry the fuck up," he spits at me.

Tears well in my eyes, wanting to escape. I take a deep breath and strip before turning my face away. I don't want to see him looking at me. Gripping my hair, he wrenches my head around, forcing me to look into his leering eyes. I watch as they darken when his free hand lowers and touches me.

My stomach turns over, overwhelming nausea bubbles up and I taste the bile in my throat. I breath rapidly to prevent the bile from erupting all over the man and fight against the powerful urge to push him away.

Something in my eyes must tell him I'm struggling not to fight and he gives me a knowing smile before leaning forward, swiping his tongue over my face and moving his lips to my ear to whisper.

"Don't worry, little pie, you're going to enjoy this." He licks the side of my face again until his mouth is almost on mine. "Fight all you want, it turns me on. You're going to love every minute of me and I'll make sure you can still feel me until the next time we meet."

I can no longer stop the tears from falling and he laughs loudly before his mouth hits my breast. His teeth latch on, his head turns, twisting my captured nipple. Pain shoots through me and I scream.

***

"Aaarrrggghhh," I scramble up the bed clutching the sheet close to my chest. The nightmare causes tears to stream from my eyes. It was all so vivid, so real, as if it was happening all over again. The pain so real, it woke me from a deep sleep.

"Sugar."

I jump at the deep voice and my eyes dart around the dim room. Sergio stands from where he'd been sitting in an armchair in the corner.

"It's okay, no-one will ever hurt you again."

Drawing my knees into my chest, I wrap the sheet around me tighter, like a security blanket. Sergio approaches the bed slowly and carefully, aware of my fear. I shrink back a little. I'm still not sure how I should feel about him, but as he comes closer, I see the pain in his eyes and it pulls at something inside me.

"Can I sit?" He points to the bed and I give permission by nodding.

Dropping down, he rests his elbows on his knees and rests his head in his hands. I watch as he breathes hard, struggling with himself, and my heart softens a little. I'm worried he's getting ready to tell me something I don't want to hear.

"Is everything okay?" I whisper.

He shakes his head. I study him closer and see the small blood spatters on his hands. I don't know what urges me to do it, but I lean forward and touch his hand. The bolt of electricity I felt earlier, zaps through me again. I don't have to ask if he felt it too, he stiffens before relaxing again and I have the answer to my unasked question.

"Are you hurt?" I whisper.

"No, sugar."

Slowly, oh so slowly and gently, he wraps his hand around mine. I feel his warmth travel through me and struggle to concentrate on something else besides what he is making me feel.

"Sugar, I need to take you somewhere safer."

"I thought you said I was safe here?" I begin trembling and Sergio rubs my hand to soothe me, but it's like my body has a mind of its own.

"You are, but not safe enough now we know who is involved. I need to take you to one of our safe houses. It's not far from here and Brooklyn can still visit."

Thoughts war in my head, am I safe with this man? Is this all a trick? Brooklyn's words about trusting them replay through my mind and I nod. "If you think it's best, I'll go with you. I trust you."

He tilts his head to the side and stares at me. "You trust me?"

Did I really say I trusted him? I haven't come close to trusting anyone in years. I close my eyes and send out a silent prayer hoping I won't regret it. But, yeah. I think I really do trust him. What the hell is going on with me? I've known this man less than twenty-four hours and I genuinely trust him. Maybe it's because he's shown me nothing but kindness and asked for nothing in return. I gaze back into those midnight eyes and a feeling so strong shoots through me. I open my mouth knowing there is only one answer to his question.

"Yes, I trust you."

Bringing my hand to his mouth, with eyes still on mine, he grazes his lips over the skin. Small goosebumps break out over me and I shiver. *What the fuck was that?*

"Grazie, Sugar."

I slide my hand from his and my stomach twists at the loss.

"Brooklyn will come up and help you get dressed and then we'll head off."

"Okay."

"I'll be back soon." He nods, pushes to his feet and gazes down at me before heading to the door. "Thank you, Sergio."

"Always, mio tesoro."

Chapter Ten

Sergio

I leave the room, allowing the door to close behind me. Brooklyn was leaning against the wall and she gave me a knowing smile.

"Miss Brooklyn, can you help Kirsty to get dressed, she may need to borrow some of your clothes?"

"Sergio, it's just Brooklyn and of course I'll help her."

"I think she needs a friend right now."

She placed her hand on my arm. "I know and I'll be there for her, and also for you, with anything you need."

"Grazie, Brooklyn." I nod while a million things flash through my mind about the hell we are about to be involved in. I'm overcome with a feeling of helplessness, a feeling I haven't had in a long time, not since Marcella. I place a hand against the wall, bend forward and take a few breaths to settle myself.

Brooklyn speaks softly. "You don't say a lot and I get that. I know events from the past haunt you, but if personal experience has taught me anything, it's that sometimes it's worth fighting for the future you want. You can't allow your demons to win." She opens the door to Kirsty's room and I glance over my shoulder in time to see the truth of her words in her eyes before she enters the room and closes the door.

Her words replay in my head and I know I would go back to hell to give my Sugar the answers she needs, even if that means facing down Paulie DeMarko again. But, this time I'll be ready for him. Pulling my phone from my pocket, I hit Theo's number and wait while it rings.

"Sergio, what can I do for you?" He sounds irritated, but I don't have time to ask why. I need him to meet me at the safe house, I'll talk to him then.

"I need you at the safe house in Warabrook and I need everything you can find on a man named Bruno J." I know it might be a long shot, but I want to start with him first and go from there.

"Si." There's silence for a moment and I think he may have disconnected the call. I'm forced to hold the phone away from my ear when he roars down the line. "What the fuck!"

When it quiets again, I move the phone back to my ear. I wonder if he's found out something already. "What is it?"

"Someone is trying to hack into my fucking system. Fuck, piece of shit. I'll meet you there, but first I need to try and stop this figlia di madre." He ends the call and I shake my head wondering what else we are up against.

I roll my shoulders in an attempt to relieve the tension, I need to do something about it, I need a drink. I make my way towards the kitchen and I'm on the stairs when my phone rings in my pocket. *Fuck what now.* I pull it out to see Dominic's number flashing on the screen.

"Boss?"

"Sergio, are you still at the house?"

"Si."

"Call Doc, Antonio has been shot in the shoulder."

"What the fuck?"

"No time to explain now, but make sure Brooklyn knows we're on our way and we have Katherine with us. Also, it may be best for Kirsty and you to be gone before we get there."

"On it, Boss." I'm about to press end when he speaks again.

"Are you ready for what's to come?" I know he's talking about Paulie DeMarko.

"I will be," I say between clenched teeth. "I have Theo meeting me at the safe house."

"Bene, call me when you find out something." Before I can answer, he ends the call.

***

I enter the safe house with Kirsty firmly in my arms and she holds onto the full bag of fluid attached to her I.V. When I look down, I see her eyes darting around, taking everything in.

"Come on, Sugar, I'll show you around before I take you to your room."

She nods. She hasn't said a word since we left Dominic's house and I don't push her to speak. I know it's a lot to take in, she's frightened and still very weak. I stride down the hallway and show her the kitchen.

"When you feel stronger, feel free to help yourself to anything you want."

Her eyes scan the room. It's spacious with numerous wooden cupboards, granite benchtops and a small sitting area is attached. I cross to the other side of the room where glass doors open into an enclosed area with a pool.

"There's an indoor pool!" Her eyes shoot around the room in an attempt to absorb everything, but I can tell she is overwhelmed.

"How about I show you more later. I'll take you up to your room so you can rest."

Leaving the kitchen area, I head towards the stairs leading up to three bedrooms and two bathrooms. We enter the master bedroom and I open the door to show her the ensuite. "I'll bring the bag of clothes Brooklyn gave you up later, is that okay?"

She nods and I notice her fidgeting with the bag of fluid in her hands. "You're tired."

"I am, sorry."

"Don't be, you need much more time to recover." I pull back the covers with one hand and lay her down before taking the bag from her. I flick up the pole from behind the headboard, I'd organized it to be fitted earlier in readiness for her coming back here, and hang the bag from the hook.

"I'll let you get comfortable. I know you're confused and what's been happening is a lot to take in, but I want you to make yourself at home here." I pull the covers over her and my heart aches when she flinches at the action. I know she has a long way to go before the reaction to people approaching her ceases.

"I promise, I'll never hurt you." I brush my lips over her forehead and hope she believes me.

I close the door and head downstairs. I hear the front door open and close and freeze for a moment, I'd forgotten to set the fucking alarm I move into the hallway, gun drawn and find Theo. I shove the gun away and give him a chin lift.

"What's with the fucking gun, fratello?"

"I forgot to set the fucking alarm" I notice how tired he looks. "You look like shit."

"Thanks, fratello, you are always so fucking nice to me."

I chuckle at his sarcasm.

"What the fuck is happening and why am I here?"

"Not here, let's go into the kitchen." As we head to the kitchen, I sigh loudly. I'm ready for this shit to end.

"Katherines back home, but her bitch of a sister has now disappeared," Theo informs me.

"Fuck."

"My thoughts exactly, fratello."

"Have you heard how Antonio is?"

"Si, I was just talking to Dominic, that's how I know about Katherine. Docs looking at him now."

"Bene."

"So, do you want to fill me in on what else is happening?" He sets up his laptop on the breakfast bar."

I tell him about how we found Kirsty and how Joey, the fucker was torturing her. I fill him on what happened at the warehouse.

"About fucking time that traditore got what was coming to him."

I nod in agreement and flick the kettle on to make coffee. I wonder what the fuck has got Theo looking like shit. "What the fuck has got you looking like you do?"

"Fuck, where do I fucking start." He chuckles but he sounds done in.

"Someone tried to plant a fucking bug in my software, trying to access my files. Stopping it was easy enough, but every time I open a new file, it's back again. I'm playing a game of fucking cat and mouse. They've left a few cryptic messages and I've spent hours trying to work out what they fucking mean." He drags his fingers through his hair, he's obviously frustrated but I don't know shit about that stuff so, I don't comment. "This morning, I finally got a name so it's a start. Now I need to go through and find where she's been in my system. I need to find what she's managed to get into and if she's left any codes. "She?" I ask confused

"Yeah, I'm only guessing, but I don't think any guy would go by the name, Trixie."

"Good point, fratello."

"Let's get into it, we don't have time to waste. This shit is big."

I hand him a coffee, he boots up his computer and we set to work on finding everything we can on Bruno J and anybody else who may be involved with him.

Chapter Eleven

Kirsty

Something has woken me. Lifting my head, I stare out the window to find it's now dark outside. I slap a hand to my mouth to cover a yawn. I must have fallen into a deep sleep. The last thing I remember was Sergio leaving to head downstairs, then I heard a door open and close and thought he'd left me alone. I began to panic, even though I knew in my heart he wouldn't leave me here with no-one, but when I heard another man's voice and Sergio asking him to follow him through to the kitchen, I relaxed.

I scan the dimly lit room and wonder what it was that woke me, then I hear it. Someone is hitting something and grunting loudly. The panic sets in again and I start shaking, I need to know Sergio is okay.

I swing my legs over the side of the bed and holding onto the backboard, push to my feet. I stand for a few moments allowing the dizziness to subside, take the almost empty bag of fluid from the pole and leave the room. I take it slowly, I'm weak and unsteady but I have to see Sergio isn't hurt. I head toward the sound and take the steps carefully. I stop when I reach the bottom and listen again. The noise is louder here and echoes around me. I head toward a door which has been left ajar, and peek through the small gap into the lit room.

Sergio has his back to me, he's hitting a punching bag over and over. I watch, mesmerized as sweat trickles over the rises and falls of hard muscles shaping his tattooed back. Warmth settles deep inside me and I feel heat creep up my neck. I lick my parched lips as he grunts out a swing and the bag flies back in the air. Placing my hand against the wall beside me, I take a deep breath in an effort to get myself under control. Holy hell my body is on fire. I close my eyes for a moment before heading towards the kitchen for a tall glass of cool water.

***

Searching the cabinets, I find a glass and fill it with water from the fridge. Turning, I lean against the cool metal of the fridge door and take a few sips of the water. I cross to the windows lining the wall to the backyard and gaze up at the bright moon high in the sky. A smile pulls at my lips and the feeling of peace I get every time I see the moon, washes over me.

I hear footsteps approaching from the direction of the hallway and turn to find a man standing in the doorway. My heart bangs with terror, it scares the shit out of me. I scream and my glass hits the floor shattering to a million pieces. The bag of fluid joins it and what was left runs out over the floor after a shard pierces the plastic.

70

"Shit, sorry, Miss." The man appears as shocked as me.

A light flickers on almost blinding me and I hear the sound of feet hitting the wooden floor as someone runs towards us. Sergio explodes into the kitchen, covered in sweat, muscles flexed ready to fight. "What the fuck happened?" he shouts.

"I'm sorry, so sorry. I didn't mean it. I didn't mean to scream and drop the glass," I sob before sliding down the wall and hugging my knees to my chest. I cower, my head lowered, waiting for the blows to come.

I feel fingers beneath my chin tilting my face up, I try not to flinch away.

"It's okay, Sugar, I've got you." Sergio sweeps me into his arms and cradles me against his hard, warm chest. A light sheen of sweat coats my fingers as I wrap my arms around his neck and bury my face against his chest. I take a few deep breaths, drawing his scent into my body to calm my racing heart.

The other man hands Sergio the remains of the empty fluid bag.

"Theo, clean that up," Sergio growls as we pass him and head towards the stairs.

"On it," he calls back.

"I'm s-s-sorry," I whisper. "Are you going to beat me?" Sergio gives me a shocked look laced with sorrow and anger.

"Sugar, I will never, for as long as I live, raise a hand to you for any reason. It's fine, it was only a glass. You're safe and that's all that matters."

I relax into him as he takes me up the stairs to my new room.

He places me gently on the bed, but I don't let him go. I feel safe for the first time in what feels like forever.

"Lay with me, hold me," I whisper and squeeze my eyes shut, not believing what I've just said.

I hear him suck in a deep breath and worry he's going to say no.

"I have to take your drip down first. Doc said it could come out as soon as you started drinking."

I nod, wondering if it is his way of saying no to me. He takes a band-aid from the side table and tears open the package then hands it me to hold while he withdraws the needle from my hand. He wraps the tubing around the bag and places it on the bedside table out of the way. After covering the wound with the band-aid, he climbs onto the bed, lays down and holds me to his chest.

"Rest mio tesoro," he whispers into my hair before kissing my forehead.

I cling to him, he's my lifeline, my safe place. Closing my eyes, I drift off.

***

Looking up at the sky, I let the cool night air refresh me, bring a dandelion puff up to my lips and blow. Closing my eyes, I make a wish like I do every time I'm out here. Opening my eyes, I watch as the little puffs float around me, wishing things were that simple and I could float away with them. Hearing the creak of the back door. I cringe, knowing I've been caught again. Most nights I'm lucky, but other nights, not so much.

"Inside, NOW!" Karen screeches.

Quickly getting to my feet, I scurry up the steps. She grabs me and I'm pushed into the house. She doesn't say a word. I know what's to come next so, as soon as I step into my room, I strip out of my nightgown and drop to my knees.

"I don't know why you think you can go out there," she sneers. "I hope you soaked it up because after tomorrow, you won't see the outside for a fucking, long time."

As her words register and she starts to flog me with the belt, I let the tears fall. Not because of the pain caused by the blows, but at the thought of not being able to see the sun or the moon again.

"To your feet," she spits out.

Climbing to my feet, I brace my hands against the old paint chipped wall and wait for what's to come next. When she runs her fingernails down the center of my back causing the sting of my wounds to intensify, I hiss out a breath and close my eyes. Her hand slides around the front of me until she's cupping me. Leaning close to the side of my face she licks up my tears and applies pressure between my legs.

"The boss will be waiting for you, he has a special present for you." She slides her hand back up the front until she's cupping my breast and dragging her nails over the bite marks scattered there.

"You like me playing with you, don't you little whore?" She grips my hair in her other hand and wrenches my head back.

I remain silent, not willing to give her any more satisfaction than what she is already getting by tormenting me.

***

"Shhh, Sugar."

I hear a deep voice and scream out, push away from the arms holding me and almost fall off the bed. A warm arm stops me from hitting the floor. I look around, frantic, trying to work out where I am. My eyes connect with his and there is so much pain. I stay focused on him until my breathing settles.

"Why are you here?" I speak softly. Something flashes in his eyes, but it's gone before I can understand what it meant.

"I'm sorry, Sugar, you were having a bad dream."

I turn away, afraid if I stay locked on his eyes, I'll cry. I remember then, I'd asked him to lay with me. When I turn back my eyes are riveted on the tattoos covering his chest.

"I'm sorry, I remember now that I asked you to lay with him. I was confused by the nightmare."

He reaches over to run his fingertips down my cheek but I stiffen and tense.

Sergio stays quiet for a moment, his eyes searching mine. "I'm going to fix some breakfast. Do you feel up to a wash and coming down or, will I bring it up?" "I think I'll be okay to come down."

He nods before standing. At his full height, bare chested, painted with glorious tattoos, my mind instantly recalls the images of him belting the punching bag last night and I feel heat creeping over me. I lower my head allowing my hair to hang like a curtain in front of my face to disguise my blushing.

I wait to hear the door close and let out the breath I was holding. My body is humming with want, but I need to pull myself together, it will do me no good to get close to this man. I climb to my feet slowly and head for the bathroom connected to the bedroom.

Chapter Twelve

Sergio

Why the fuck did you stay in there all night, you fucking cazzo? I shake my head, but can't get past the fact, she belongs in my arms. It felt so fucking right having her tiny body wrapped around me, her head resting on my bare chest. Running my fingers through her dark hair calmed me like nothing else ever has. But, to see that look of terror in her eyes when she didn't remember where she was or, the small cries and whimpers which sounded while she was sleeping, had me wanting to kill any motherfucker who'd either hurt her before or threatened to hurt her in the future. It pissed me off that I couldn't do a fucking thing, how can I fight something I can't see?

"Fuck!" I enter the kitchen scrubbing my hands over my face.

"What's up, fratello?"

I swing around to find Theo sitting at the table drinking coffee, I wonder if he's had any sleep at all.

"Nothing." I grunt as I cross the kitchen and flick on the kettle before turning. "Scusa, fratello." I apologize for being an asshole and snapping at him.

"Si, we're good. Is your girl okay? I heard her scream."

"Honestly, I don't fucking know. I think she's reliving everything in her dreams."

"Fanculo (fuck)."

"My thoughts exactly. It's so hard watching her suffer through it all again." I run a hand over my head. "Did you find anything?" I need a diversion from witnessing Kirsty's nightmare.

"Si, but you better make yourself a cup of coffee first."

"Si, you good?" I look down to his cup.

"Si."

"Did you get any sleep?"

"A few hours but something was bugging me so, I had to look into it."

"To do with Bruno J or something else?"

"Mostly Bruno J, but I think I've figured out how to crack Trixie's messages."

"Bene."

There's not a lot that gets past Theo when it comes to computers, he has to be one of the best hackers in the world. I knew this girl's cryptic messages would have gotten to him and he wouldn't rest until he'd worked it all out.

I lower slices of bread into the toaster and make two coffees. I'm not sure how Kirsty likes it or if she even drinks it, but it's there if she wants it. I take a chance and make it the same as mine, two sugars and milk. I turn towards the doorway when I hear footsteps and see Kirsty come to an abrupt stop when she notices Theo is here too.

"Sugar, this is Theo. Theo, meet Kirsty."

"Hello." She speaks quietly as she looks at her feet.

"I'm sorry about scaring you last night, Miss Kirsty."

Her head lifts and she looks towards Theo, she studies him for a moment. Jealousy twists my stomach but I try to push it away, I'm sure she doesn't need my caveman ass right now.

"I should be the one who's sorry." I can't help thinking she has the soft voice of an angel.

I look towards Theo and see his eyebrows drawn in confusion. "Miss Kirsty, you have nothing to apologize for.

I watch as surprise flashes across her face before she nods and pads towards me. I place the toast on a plate on the bench, grab her coffee and place it next to the plate.

"We don't have a lot in the cupboard at the moment, but I found strawberry jam in the fridge. I hope that's okay. I made coffee but if it's not how you like it, I can make another."

"Thank you." She hoists herself onto a stool at the bench, picks up her mug, takes a sip of the hot brew and screws up her beautiful face. She looks at me and I bite my lip to stop the chuckle which wants to escape. Turning, I pour her a glass of water and place it down in front of her just in case.

"You don't have to drink the coffee, Sugar."

She takes another sip while watching me over the rim of the mug. Her eyes shine and I find myself unable to look away.

"I guess I can get use to this, it's really not bad." A slight smile hits her lips and I wonder what it would be like to see a full smile light up her face. I can't seem to control myself as I reach over and gently touch the side of her mouth when I see a small dimple appear. I realize what I have done when she freezes and I quickly pull my hand back.

"I'm sorry." I turn my back to her when I feel my cock becoming hard as fuck. I barely slept all night thanks to having a perpetual hard-on, but at least when she was asleep, I could hide it. *Fuck get your shit together.* I excuse myself, leave the room and head up the stairs to the bathroom. I need to cool my ass down.

***

Closing the bathroom door, I flick the lock and drop my shorts. I run my hand up my hard length and squeeze. Closing my eyes, I picture Kirsty laying in my arms, her sweet scent surrounding me and bite my lip to stop a moan slipping out. Stepping into the shower, I flick the tap on cold. The water hits my chest and flows down the front of me, chilling my body. I hope like hell, I can pull myself together before I lose control and scare the shit out of my girl. Resting my hands against the tiled wall, I drop my head and let the water pound against me. I squeeze my eyes shut and imagine Kirsty in the shower with me, Picturing the water running over her curves, my tongue trying to catch every droplet. I growl in the back of my throat as I imagine rubbing soap all over her silky soft skin, down to her luscious ass. Taking a few deep breaths, I grab the soap and run it over my chest. I fantasize it's Kirsty's hand instead of mine and that does it. I lose all control and have to grip myself as I come hard all over the shower wall. I groan as I come hard, black dots appear in my vision and my knees shake.

"Fuck. Fuck. Fuck." Breathing deeply, I rest my head against the cool tiles and slam my hand against it when I realize I didn't need to jerk off to come. Her image was enough to bring me to my knees. Taking a moment so I can get my bearings back, I finish washing and clean the shower wall. Stepping out, I wrap a towel around my waist. Bending forward, I look at myself in the mirror. I have to regain control of myself, she's been through enough to last a lifetime and she doesn't need my uncontrollable ass all over her. After toweling myself off, I grab the clothes I'd put in here after my workout last night and throw them on. I need to get back downstairs, see what Theo has found out and make sure Kirsty at least tries to eat something.

Chapter Thirteen

Kirsty

I'm not exactly sure what just happened but I saw the moment I froze in his eyes. I didn't mean to, it's reflexive, but as the tip of his finger touched my cheek I felt something zip through me and the nervousness of Theo being here disappeared. How can one simple touch set off so many emotions when for so long I haven't wanted anybody to touch me and when they did, I blocked it out? One simple touch from this tatted up mountain of a man has me wanting to beg for more. I jump when music starts to play and swing around to see the television is on.

"I didn't mean to startle you, but it was too quiet and I need background noise when I'm working," Theo says with an apologetic look on his face.

"It's okay," I whisper before turning back to my food. I pick up a piece of toast and take a bite, closing my eyes when the taste of strawberries explodes in my mouth. It's been so long since I've tasted anything so good, not since I was taken. I'm used to water and plain food like rice or bread. I must have moaned at the taste and hear a low chuckle. I feel the heat creep up my neck, not wanting to turn around, I fix my eyes on the plate.

"I'm sorry, Miss Kirsty."

I feel bad that he thinks he needs to apologize, that he thinks he has done something wrong. I focus on the plate and explain. "It's okay, you have no reason to be sorry. It's been many years since I've tasted something so good."

Silence hangs between us before Theo asks, "How long?"

"Um.. shit, um..." I'm not sure if I should tell him.

"You don't have to tell me, but the more I know, the better my chances of finding something that may help."

I'm confused by his words, his offer to, but I answer him anyway.

"About ten years." The only sound for a moment is the music in the background.

"Fuck," he growls.

I'm not sure I want to answer anything else he might ask. I jump off my stool, grab the glass of water and make my way towards the back door. I want to enjoy the fresh air and sit in the sun for a little bit. I stop in my tracks when he speaks again.

"I'm sorry this happened to you."

I nod, not knowing what to say. I'm sorry too because no matter what happens next, I'll never get those ten years back. Pushing through the back door, I make my way onto the lush green lawn and sit down. I look around and see patches of dandelions, a smile pulls at my lips. Reaching over I grab one and study the white puff. Playing with it in my fingers, I can't help feeling that maybe all the times I wished for survival and a normal life, maybe it was what brought me Sergio. He's not a white knight riding in and saving the day, but a man with a kind heart who swept me into his arms and saved me from the life which had been forced on me.

Gazing into the bright sun, I bathe in the rays warming my skin. I take a deep breath and soak it all in, being here is almost surreal. I hear a voice from inside, it's one I don't recognize. I shake my head when it dawns on me, it's a voice from the television announcing the next song *—I want to know what love is* by *Foreigner.* The music floats through the air and I fall back to the grass and listen to the words. The lyrics flow through my muddled mind and I question whether I will ever know what love is.

It's hard thinking you are in a home filled with love, only to be given away on your fifteenth birthday after being told you were only born to repay a debt.

A tear slides down my cheek but I quickly wipe it away. I turn my attention back to the sun and clear blue sky, not wanting to think about the why's and what if's. It's time I took back control and if everything Sergio has been saying is true, this is a place where I can do that. Somewhere safe where I can prove to myself, and everybody else, that I'm stronger than the marks on my body. I can overcome the words which were thrown at me, the taunting and cruelty. I glance down at my chest, at the bandages there and promise myself one thing - I will not be that person again. I roll to the side and pluck out another dandelion. Closing my eyes, I wish for strength and the willpower to never look back, to always push forward. I open my eyes and watch as the puff's float away in the light breeze.

***

"What are you doing Sugar?" His voice comes from behind me and I jump at the sound. I was so caught up in my own head, I hadn't realized he was standing close by.

"I'm sorry." I scramble to my feet, but I don't bow my head in terror. Instead, I lock eyes with him and dare him to tell me I can't be out here.

"You have no reason to be sorry, I told you last night to treat this place as your own."

I open and close my mouth, not sure what to say to that. I'd been ready to do battle with him.

"Do you want to sit back down?"

I nod and sit, but I don't relax as I watch his eyes track everything I'm doing. He sits next to me and I try not to flinch away.

"I'm sorry the lawn hasn't been mowed, I'll get Demetri to come over this arvo if you want." He waves his arms in the air as he speaks.

"It's fine."

"Si." He nods "But, if you want to lay out here I would rather you be comfortable and not be laying on weeds." He points towards the dandelion patches.

I feel a sudden panic at their possible loss and grip his arm. I try to ignore the rush which hits me when I touch him. "Please don't cut them, they aren't weeds, they're dandelions."

He glances down at my hand for a moment before covering it with his own larger hand. He squeezes a little and I think he's going to move it, but he leaves it there and warmth floods me. When I gaze into his eyes, they are shining and the intensity reaches deep inside me.

"Why does it matter if they are cut?"

"They're like little wishes." I snap my mouth shut and peer at my lap when I realize I've spoken aloud. *Shit I can't seem to control my mouth this morning.* I feel his fingers on my chin and fight the need to pull away. I lock eyes with him and notice how soft they have become. Dropping his hand back over mine, I realize I still haven't let him go.

"It's okay, Sugar, can you show me how it works?" He smiles and my stomach performs summersaults. Nodding, I reach over with my free hand and pick one up. "You bring it to your mouth like this..." I raise the white puff to my lips. "...close your eyes, make a wish or think of something you want to happen and then blow." I blow out a deep breath.

When I open my eyes and look towards Sergio, there is a strange expression on his face and his eyes are fixed in the region of my mouth. I lick my lips and wonder what it would be like to be kissed by this incredible man. From the corner of my eye, I see his hand reach towards me. I don't move, stiffen or flinch, instead I sit calmly while he runs the tips of his fingers down the side of my face.

"You're a beautiful woman, but when you smile and this dimple appears..." he touches said dimple before running his finger across my bottom lip. "....you take my breath away."

Well, that knocks the wind from me. No-one has ever spoken to me that way. When he removes his finger, I feel my lips tingle and suck it into my mouth. I want the feeling to last forever.

"I'm sorry, Sugar." He blows out a deep breath. "I won't touch you again without asking. I just can't seem to be near you without wanting to have you in my arms." Without another word, he stands and heads towards the back door.

I don't know what to say, I seem to have this problem a lot when he's around. I stay silent. Where the hell would I begin to explain to this man what he does to me? Laying back on the grass, I close my eyes and wonder if what I'm feeling is real or just my head telling me to latch on to this man who has shown me kindness for the first time in years.

After burying my feelings for so long, refusing to allow them to come to the surface, can I allow myself to start feeling now? I'm confused, the only thing which is clear to me right now is, I need to get stronger. I need to take things one step at a time.

Chapter Fourteen

Sergio

I let the screen door close under its own weight and stand peering back out to the yard. Kirsty is lying on her back, staring up at the sky, the hint of a smile on her face. It's obvious she's not used to being outdoors, I guess she probably would have been in deep shit if she'd been caught outside.

"Is she okay?" Theo asks from behind me.

"Yeah, she's just enjoying the sun."

"Sergio, she spoke to me before she went outside."

I turn to face him. "And?"

"They had her for ten fucking years." The way he growls, it's not hard to hear he's angry.

I feel anger well within, rage at the thought of what they did to her when she was still only a kid. Marcella flashes into my thoughts and the last time I saw her alive. I couldn't do shit to save her, but I sure as fuck can make sure nobody touches my girl again.

"You said you found something?" I change the subject needing to calm the anger swirling within.

"Si." He nods and we move to where he has his computer set up. He takes a seat at the table, clicks a few keys and looks up at me.

I round the table to see the screen showing the picture of a pudgy little man, probably in his late fifties and with next to no hair.

"Bruno J." Theo taps the screen with his finger.

"Piece of shit!"

"Si, Fratello. I managed to find this and a few newspaper articles about him. I'm still searching for his last known whereabouts. He was last arrested in 2008, made bail and appears to have vanished. I'll search until I find him."

"Bene." I study the screen, committing his face to memory. When I hear the screen door close, I glance up to see Kirsty has entered the house.

"I'll go up to my room." Her voice is agonizingly soft.

I clench my fists, determined someone will pay for the harm done to my woman.

"Si, Sugar. I spoke with Doc earlier and he'll be here in a few hours to check you over."

"Okay." Her head is bowed as she walks from the kitchen.

I rub my hands down my face before dragging one through my hair, a piece of dandelion catches my finger.

Visions of how she looked when she held it to her mouth and the peace which seemed to wash over her, fill my mind. I want nothing more than to see that look of calm on her face every day for the rest of our lives.

Watching her knocked the air from my lungs, I wanted so badly to kiss her but, it's too soon and I can't betray her trust in that way. The last thing on her mind is being mine. I need to clear these thoughts and focus on finding the assholes who did this to her.

***

It's been two fucking weeks and we still can't find a damn thing on that cazzo, Bruno J. Kirsty barely speaks a word about what happened to her and I don't want to push her but we are coming up empty without her help.

Dominic is demanding answers I can't give him. Theo is working his ass off but, despite having tried everything he can think of there's still nothing. We've hit a brick wall and I hate that I can't give Kirsty the peace she fucking deserves.

I hit the bag harder, sweat drips down my face but it's not enough to settle this anger within me. It's fucking killing me to keep my distance from her, I haven't touched her since the day in the back yard. I feel like an addict needing a fix and have to keep reminding myself, I can't do anything to confuse her anymore than she already is. But, fuck, her sweet scent hangs in the air around me and I'm hanging on by a thread. I'm not sure how many nights I've gone to bed hard as fucking steel or how many times I've dreamed about that first night with her sleeping in my arms.

I hear her whimpers and cries in the dark of night but, like tonight, I can't do shit about it. So, I'm down here hitting this fucking bag to stop myself from going into her room, gathering her into my arms and just fucking holding her.

"Fuck," I growl before lashing out left, right and center. I don't give a shit about technique, I'm just fucking hitting.

I'm not sure how long I've been down here but, my arms feel heavy as fuck. I stop the movement of the bag and lean my head against it, sucking in gulps of air.

"Sergio."

I swing around at the sound of her soft voice.

"Sugar."

We stand staring at each other, not moving, not speaking, just staring. She's a fucking vision of loveliness, her long hair swept up in a messy knot on top of her head and wearing a pair of sweats and a shirt which Brooklyn gave her.

"I can't sleep," she whispers.

Her eyes roam over my body.

I feel myself harden, turn away to grab the towel off the seat in the corner and the water bottle. I try to focus my attention anywhere except on her. I guzzle down the water, wipe the sweat from my forehead, compose myself and turn back around.

"Would you like to lie under the stars?" I know she loves being outside, it's when she's at her happiest so, I had Nico and Demetri bring over a daybed today so she could spend as much time out there as she wanted.

I always left her alone but would watch from my bedroom window. She'd smile up at the sky, the sun, the moon as if seeing it all for the first time. Fuck it makes me angry knowing she was denied this simple pleasure.

When she'd fall asleep under the stars, I worried about her getting sick so, I'd pick her up and carry her into her bed. At first she would startle and shy away but for the past week, she hasn't woken and she actually snuggles against me.

"Yes."

"Si, but it's cool so if you fall asleep I'll bring you back inside." I drop the towel and water bottle and head back to the bag. It's going to be a very long night.

"Will you lie with me?" Her voice is so soft I barely hear her.

Before she can change her mind, I nod and move closer to her. I follow behind when she heads for the kitchen door which leads into the back yard. She heads straight for the bed while I start to grab a chair from the veranda.

She turns to see what I'm doing. "I want you to hold me. Please?"

I suck in a breath and gaze deep into her eyes, I need to make sure she understands what she's asking. Her eyes sparkle in the moonlight, there's a peace and calm I haven't seen there before. I let go of the chair and head for the bed with her. When she reaches for my hand, the now familiar warmth from her touch shoots through me.

I climb onto the bed and lie on my side, she lies down on her back beside me.

"Doesn't the sight take your breath away?"

91

She's talking about the stars and moon, I'm talking about her when I answer. "Si, it does.

She turns to find my eyes fixed on her and knows it was her I had in mind. She sucks in a deep breath. I remain still when she reaches out and runs her fingertips along the side of my face.

"Earlier, when I was upstairs and trying to sleep, I realized something."

I remain quiet when she pauses.

"I look into your eyes and they're so kind, I feel like I'm awake for the first time in my life, not trapped in a nightmare. I never want that feeling to end."

"Sugar." She runs her fingers over my lips to stop me from speaking.

"I'm not sure when I'll be ready for sex..."

I open my mouth but she shakes her head.

"I spoke with Brooklyn about how I feel when I'm around you and she kinda sorted out all the muddled-up things in my head. I know t's not fair of me but, having you touch me the way you do is about all I can handle for now. Oh, and this."

She leans up and places her lips over mine, I freeze for a moment when I feel softness. Snapping out of my shock, I move my hand to behind her head and graze her bottom lip with my tongue. When she gasps, I take the opportunity to slip inside. I groan at the sweetest thing I have ever tasted, it's as if pure sugar shoots through my veins.

Kirsty moans, I pull back and rest my forehead against hers while we both catch our breath.

"Sugar, I don't care if this is all we *ever* have."

"What?" Her question comes out breathy.

"Knowing I can have your touch is enough for me but, I know when you're ready you'll tell me."

"What if I'm never ready?

I kiss her forehead and she squeezes her eyes shut.

"Sugar, I just need your touch, I'm lost without it. This right here, what we're doing, it centers me."

I watch as a smile curls her lips.

"Hold me, Sergio."

"Always tesoro mio." I lay back on the bed, wrap my arm around her waist and she settles against my bare chest. I gaze up at the stars and can't help but feel content for the first time in what feels like forever. Having her in my arms is all I need.

Chapter Fifteen

Kirsty

My eyes flicker open when bright rays of sunlight stream through the window. I snuggle back against the warmth and safety of Sergio's hard chest and my thoughts drift to last night, the stars above, his arms wrapped around me. Protecting me.

It took me all afternoon and a conversation with Brooklyn to start seeing what was right in front of me the whole time.

Does it mean I'm not scared anymore? Fuck, no. I'm still scared. Terrified I'll wake up back in Hell and find this has all been a beautiful dream. I'm also worried I won't be able to let Sergio completely in but, if what we have now is all it can be, I can live with it. As my touch centers him, his centers me.

I reflect on the conversation with Brooklyn again.....

"How are you feeling today?" Brooklyn asked as she places shopping bags on my bed.

"I don't know." I answer honestly and shake my head.

"What don't you know? Has Doc been by?"

"Yeah, he said I was fully healed but I may have some scarring." I shrug my shoulders knowing full well I'll have scars.

"We all have scars, Kirsty but we learn to not let them hold us back."

I glance at her leg when I remember her telling me last week what had happened to her. How Dominic had saved Brooklyn and her daughter from her ex. Knowing what she's been through made me feel less alone, made me realize other people deal with hard shit too. I'm not stupid, I know I'm not the only one in the world who has been through hell and to talk with someone who has also lived through a nightmare, makes it a little easier to deal with my demons. I don't feel like a freak. Knowing Dominic stood by and helped Brooklyn makes me understand this is what Sergio is trying to do for me.

"How much longer do you need the cane for?"

"Doc said another week and I should be good. Thank fuck because it's starting to piss me off." She laughs and I laugh with her.

God, it feels good to laugh. We sit in silence for a few moments, side by side on the bed.

"How are you and Sergio going?"

"There's nothing going on between us although I suspect he would like it if there was." I shrug "He's been keeping his distance because he senses it's what I need. It's for the best, I guess."

"How is it for the best?"

I peer at her and wonder if she really understands what I've been through if she's asking this question.

"Don't look at me like that." She shakes her head at me and I'm confused. "What I'm trying to say is, Sergio wants to be there for you and he would never do anything to hurt you. Forget what he does for a living and see the man who has been with you from the beginning"

I remember when Brooklyn explained about her ex and said Dominic was a Mafia boss. She didn't say what Sergio does but she did say he was a part of the family. I was frightened at first until Brooklyn reminded me they are good men. They would never hurt me or any other woman and they hate anyone who does. I hear what she's saying but would Sergio be willing to stay by me if I could never let him touch me in that way?

"I guess that's what I'm confused about, wouldn't he have expectations like any other man?" I look down at my lap and fidget with the end of my shirt.

"Kirsty, he would never force you to do anything you didn't want to or feel comfortable with. You need to talk to him, tell him what it is you want. He knows how badly you've been hurt and I think he's waiting for you to be ready to go to him."

"I think I love him." My voice sounds dreamy even to my ears, I slap my hands over my mouth wishing I'd never said that. "Fuck, I'm so confused," I mumble into my hands. The last thing I expected was for Brooklyn to laugh at me

"I'm sorry I didn't mean to laugh but I don't think I have ever heard you swear before." She wraps her arm around me and gives me a sideways hug. Normally I freeze when anyone touches me but I have kind of gotten used to Brooklyn.

"As far as you loving him, that's a good thing because he loves you too."

"What?" Surely she's not serious, how could he love me?

"Honey, you need to know when the Grasso men see the woman they want, they fall hard and fast. It doesn't matter what anybody does, or says, nothing will get in their way of taking what's theirs."

"T- t- theirs?" I stammer out. I wait for my body to start shaking but, it doesn't.

"Sergio loves you, Kirsty. Everyone saw it from the first time he brought you to the house, the way he looked at you with such sorrow and passion. He'll give you the space and time you need but know this — while you're his, he is also yours."

"Mine?"

"Yeah, honey, yours. I know those words may scare you but he will protect you, love you like nobody ever has and he will lay his life on the line for you in a heartbeat. So, try not to let the words scare you off and just let yourself feel."

"Isn't it too soon to have these feelings?"

"I don't think so, I knew after a week with Dom that he was mine and I was his."

"A week?"

I'd seen the look Brooklyn was talking about in Sergio's eyes last night and I knew I would kick myself if I didn't let my feelings surface. I turn my head and plant a light kiss in the center of Sergio's hard chest, his muscles flinch beneath my lips. I start to turn away, worried I have woken him up, when I feel his hand sliding in my hair.

"I'm sorry I woke you," I whisper.

"Sugar, never be sorry." His sleepy voice sounds sexy and sends tingles racing through me. I sit up and cower away when I feel his hand slide down my back, I can't bear for him to feel my scars.

"Sugar, are you okay?"

"Yes, I'm fine. I'm not used to waking up with someone in my bed," I lie.

"Kirsty, please look at me."

He places fingers under my chin and I turn back to face him, eyes filled with care stare back at me. "Sugar, I've seen your back before." He speaks softly and I hear the pain in his voice.

A tear slides down my cheek and I quickly swipe it away. He takes my arm and pulls me to lie back down with him, enough to let me know he doesn't want me to leave but not too hard so I know I can leave if I want to. I rest my head on his chest again and let the slow up and down motion of his breathing soothe me.

"Sugar, I have scars too. You never have to be ashamed of them with me."

"You do?"

"Yeah but how about we have some breakfast and I'll show you later."

I open my mouth to answer just as the doorbell sounds. Sergio growls, I guess he doesn't like being disturbed. He growls a lot but instead of it scaring me, it sends my senses into a spin.

"That will be Dominic and Brooklyn."

I sit up excited. "Do you think Brooklyn will have brought Evie with her this time?" I haven't met her yet and Brooklyn says she's excited to meet me.

"Not sure, Sugar but, I better get up and let them in before they break down the door." He leans over and kisses the top of my head before he climbs from the bed.

"I'll be down soon, I just want to grab a shower."

"Si, Tesoro but, if Evie is here you better not be too long. That little girl is like the *Energizer* bunny." He laughs and I giggle at the image.

He leans over me and I remain still as he grazes his lips over and whispers, "I love the sound of you giggling, I want to hear it a lot more."

I close my eyes and soak him in, his scent, his presence. When he leaves the room, I feel the loss and open my eyes.

Oh dear, what this man is doing to me? I slide to my feet and head for the shower.

Chapter Sixteen

Sergio

I head down the steps feeling lighter after last night, having my girl wrapped in my arms. I know there are things we need to talk about but I'm confident, given time, we'll get there. Last night was a huge step for her and I wasn't lying when I said as long as I had her in my arms, it would be enough.

I open the door and it's lucky I have lightning fast reactions. Evie barrels in and screams out, "Zio" (Uncle), before catapulting into my arms. I laugh at her excitement.

"Principessa Evie, have you grown since I last saw you?"

She places her small hands to the sides of my face and laughs. "No, silly."

I'm laughing when I glance to the door and watch as Dominic leads Brooklyn inside.

"Boss." I lift my chin in greeting.

He has a serious expression on his face and I wonder what the hell has happened now. I look to Brooklyn.

"Miss Brooklyn, good morning."

"Good morning, Sergio. Evie and I are going to make everyone breakfast while you two talk."

Dominic lifts Evie from my arms and kisses her cheek before placing her onto the floor.

We stay quiet, watching as the girls head to the kitchen. I wait until they are out of hearing range before speaking.

"What's happened, Boss?"

"Theo called when we were on our way over, he has something to show us."

"Do you want to wait in the office or the kitchen?"

"Let's grab a coffee while we wait." Dominic suggests.

"Si. Kirsty will be down in a moment."

"How is everything between you two?"

I smile when I think about last night. "Bene, Boss. We're taking it day by day."

"Bene, Sergio, I'm glad something is finally going right at the moment." He slaps me on the back as we head for the kitchen. I know the girls have made themselves at home when I hear music playing.

When we step into the kitchen, we find Evie sitting on the counter swinging her legs back and forth while Brooklyn rummages in the cupboards.

"Zio, when do I get to meet Aunty Kirsty?" Evie asks.

I open and close my mouth, resembling a fish taking in air. I'm unsure what to say about Evie calling Kirsty Aunty. I glance at Dominic, big help he is, he shrugs and chuckles before wrapping his arm around Brooklyn's waist.

"Princess..." It's all I get time for because Kirsty enters the room.

"Hi, you must be Evie," she says at she crosses the room to her.

Evie nods and smiles. "Ooh, you're so pretty. Mummy, isn't Aunty Kirsty pretty?"

"Yes sweetpea, she sure is. How about you come and help me while Kirsty has a coffee and then we can all chat."

I look at my girl, she's peering down at her feet and I wonder what's going through her mind right now. Dom lifts Evie down from the bench and places her onto her feet.

"Be good for momma while I talk with zio."

"Okay, Papa." She looks up at Dom and gives him a megawatt smile and I see him visibly melt. He kneels down and gives her a hug and kiss. She has him wrapped around her tiny finger, he'll never be able to refuse her anything.

We head for the living room to talk and I chuckle as he shakes his head.

"You know you're fucked when she gets older, Boss."

"Sergio, I'm already fucked."

"Don't start with that shit again, Dominic," Brooklyn calls out.

I wonder what the fuck she's talking about. Dom turns to me and shakes his head. Once seated in the living room I ask, "what was that about?"

"A punk kid kissed Evie at school."

I glance toward Brooklyn in the kitchen, she catches my eye and starts to laugh before returning to whatever she was doing.

"Fanculo," I growl.

"Si, but my sweet Angel thinks I'm being over protective."

He raises his voice slightly to make sure Brooklyn hears him, she laughs louder. I watch as she whispers something to Kirsty which starts her laughing. My body reacts to the beautiful sound.

"Si, Boss, you're fucked." I turn back to him and laugh. He'll never get the upper hand with his women.

I hear the front door open and Theo walks in with a laptop under his arm. I lift my chin as he walks over to the table and puts the computer down. "Morning."

"Boss, Sergio, we need to talk."

"Theo, do you want pancakes," Brooklyn asks.

His eyes light up. "Si, Miss Brooklyn. Grazie."

"Then, move the laptop please."

"Si, Miss Brooklyn." He quickly picks it up and moves it to the living room. Dominic and I chuckle.

***

While the girls clean up after breakfast, I take the chance to observe Kirsty and make sure she's okay. Miss Evie has been like a shadow all morning and Kirsty seems to be enjoying it. She seems relaxed and at peace.

"Do we need to do this in private?" Dominic nods toward the girls as he speaks to Theo.

"Nah, Boss. I kinda need Kirsty to have a look at something for me. Sergio, I hope you don't mind us invading your home but, I've also called and asked Antonio to come over. He should be here soon."

"Shit, what did you find?" Dom sounds worried and so am I.

Theo glances toward the girls but they're too busy talking to pay us any attention. "I also need Miss Katherine to take a look at something too, I may have found something she'll want to know."

Right on cue, the doorbell rings and I push to my feet. It's turning into a fucking party around here. I head for the door but I shouldn't have bothered, Antonio has let himself in.

"Capo Bastone."

"Sergio fratello." I shake his hand and note Miss Katherine standing behind him. "Miss Katherine congratulations on the engagement."

"Thank you, Sergio, I'm guessing this big lug told you. I swear he doesn't know how to keep his mouth shut."

Antonio growls but, it's playful and he wraps his arms around her waist drawing her back into his chest.

"Si," I laugh. "Come on everyone is in the kitchen."

"Do I get to meet your girl?" Katherine asks.

I nod, loving the sound of people calling her *my girl*.

I stop at the breakfast bar when Kirsty looks over and sees Antonio and Kat behind me, alarm flashes in her eyes before recognition takes over.

"Sugar, you've met Antonio." I indicate Kat. "This is his fiancé, Katherine."

She drops her eyes to her feet, I reach over and lift her chin so she looks me in eyes.

"Are you okay Sugar?"

I watch as her eyes soften and she nods, the way she gazes at me makes me feel like we're the only ones in the room. "Do you need to lie down?" I brush my fingertips over her cheek and she leans into my touch before lifting her hand and squeezing my fingers.

"I'm okay, I promise."

"Don't worry, Sergio, go over and make yourself useful with the boys. I've got this," Katherine assures me.

I nod, knowing she will be fine with them when a smile touches Kirsty's lips.

Chapter Seventeen

Kirsty

I suck in a deep breath and let it out slowly while I watch the men step over to Theo who is setting his laptop up on the table. Something is going on and an uneasy feeling turns my stomach. I note Antonio's arm is in a sling and wonder what happened to him. Last time I saw him was in the warehouse and I wonder if Joey is responsible for his injury.

I glance at Katherine when she gives Brooklyn a hug, her baby bump a loving rub and leans against the bench to chat. Was she the girl the men were searching for when they found me?

"Kirsty," Brooklyn speaks softly but it draws me away from my thoughts.

"Sorry, I zoned out for a moment."

Her eyes soften as she looks at me. "Would you like more coffee?"

I shake my head. "No, thank you. I might just have water." I start to push up from my seat when Katherine stops me.

"Stay there, I'll get it for you."

"It's okay, I can....." Before I can finish my sentence, a glass is placed before me.

"It's fine, I kind of do this for a living." She laughs at what must be my puzzled expression. It's such a joyful, kind laugh.

"I own a café."

Brooklyn turns with two cups of coffee in her hands and places them on the bench before grabbing orange juice for Evie. The child hasn't left my side all morning.

"Is Gwen there now?" Brooklyn asks.

"Yeah. God that woman is amazing, I think Henry is helping her out today."

I have no idea who they're talking about but from what Brooklyn and Kat — she asked me to call her that — explain, they sound like wonderful people. I wish I'd had people like them as parents, my life would have turned out very different.

"Nanna Gwen and I bake every time I visit." Evie is standing beside me and I can't help but laugh at the dreamy look on her face.

"I'm guessing you make all kinds of yummy things."

"Oh, yeah." She sighs which has us all laughing.

"Kitten," a deep voice calls.

"What's up, Stud?" Kat answers.

Brooklyn leans over and whispers in my ear. "Kitten is Antonio's nickname for her.

I recall Dominic calling Brooklyn, Angel and come to the conclusion, all the men come up with affectionate nicknames for their women. I guess it's why Sergio calls me Sugar.

"Come over here for a moment, Theo wants to show you something," Antonio says.

Kat's brows knit together before she nods and moves to the men at the table.

Brooklyn smiles at her daughter. "Evie, why don't you go off and play, sweetheart." Evie jumps down from the stool next to me and heads for a small bag near the television. She pulls out a coloring book and crayons.

Brooklyn wipes her hand on a cloth and moves to Katherine's side who has silent tears pouring over her cheeks. She turns into Antonio's chest and he rubs his hand over her back soothingly. What the hell just happened?

Curiosity gets the better of me, I want to know what it was that made her cry. I get to my feet and move toward Sergio. He has his arms crossed over his chest but as I move to his side, he drops them and wraps one around my waist. He leans down close to my ear so only I can hear what he says.

"We think we found her father."

I nod before resting my head on his chest, the tone of his voice makes me think this isn't a good thing. His next words confirm my thoughts.

"He isn't a good man, Sugar."

"Miss Katherine, it looks like he's in Sydney," Theo says.

Dominic asks, "how did you find him?"

I glance at the computer screen in time to see Theo click out of what looked like a profile report and when a new image comes up on the screen, I freeze. I can hear my heart thumping loudly in my ears. I feel like I'm in a tunnel. Someone is yelling, I think it's me. Tears stream over my face. I close my eyes and try to breathe but it feels like there's a lead weight on my chest.

"Kirsty." Sergio's voice is laced with concern.

When I open my eyes, I see the panic on his face. I shake my head, take a few steps back and sink to the floor.

Sergio crouches in front of me. "Talk to me, Sugar."

"T...t-that's...." I take a deep breath as images flash through my mind and I close my eyes trying to stop them.

"Angel take Evie outside please." I hear Dominic call out in the background.

Sergio lifts me up and into his warm chest, I breath in his scent trying hard to calm down.

He leans over and whispers in my ear. "Talk to me, Sugar."

"T...thats Bruno J!" I gasp out and look up into his dark eyes.

I see the change in his eyes the moment he realizes what I've said and I tense when he curses in Italian. He turns and says something to everyone else and Katherine is crying louder.

I'm struggling to breathe and I'm trembling all over. "Breathe, Sugar."

Listening to his deep husky voice whispering in my ear starts to calm me as I allow it to seep into my bones. The trembling eases, my hands rest on his chest, feeling the steady thump of his heart and I find my voice.

"I'm sorry," I whisper.

"You have nothing to be sorry for."

"I'm okay now. Seeing his picture shook me, I wasn't expecting it."

I think about what happened, the conversation before I had my meltdown and something clicks into place. I swing around to face Kat and see realization flash in her eyes when it comes to me.

"He's your father?" I whisper.

She nods. "I promise you, I didn't know. He left when I was a little girl." She sobs in distress.

I notice everyone in the room is as shocked as me, they haven't been keeping anything from me.

"I'm so sorry, Kirsty. I swear I didn't know." Katherine's eyes plead with me to understand, to believe her but it's unnecessary.

I can see this knowledge has shocked and hurt her too. She approaches me slowly, tears stream down our faces and she wraps me in her arms. I stiffen at first before relaxing and hugging her back while we both cry.

"I promise you I didn't know," she whispers in my ear.

"I believe you."

The tension eases between us. I hear a sniff and glance over Kat's shoulder to see tears streaming over Brooklyn's cheeks before Dominic folds her into his arms.

       I fill with anger at the thought of what this monster has done not only to me, but also to these girls who are fast becoming my friends. Friends I had dreamed about over the years.

Chapter Eighteen

Sergio

Fucken shit, how did I not recognize Bruno J from the picture Theo showed me two weeks ago and why did he not run this past me first? I look to Theo and narrow my eyes. I'm fucking pissed and if the deep swallow and wide-eyed look he gives me is an indication, he fucking knows it too. My muscles clench, fists form and adrenaline is coursing through, surfing on a wave of my anger. As much as I'd like to punch Theo in the face, I won't.

I glance to where Kirsty is hugging Kat and can only fucking imagine what is going through both girls minds right now.

Brooklyn crosses to them and places her hand on Kat's arm. "Come on, how bout we all go upstairs." They nod, move apart and swipe at their damp eyes.

"Angel take princess with you," Dominic says.

Brooklyn moves to the living room where Evie's coloring book and Crayons remain on the floor. When she bends over to pick them up, Dominic stops her.

"Go and fetch Evie, Angel, I'll get these."

Brooklyn stands on tiptoes and kisses his cheek before heading to the back door and calling for her daughter.

"Sugar, do you want a glass or water or something to eat before you go upstairs?" I ask Kirsty.

She shakes her head before glancing around the room, her and Kat leave and I see Brooklyn following behind them with Evie. None of us men say a word until we hear a door closing upstairs.

"How the fuck did you find him?" Dominic demands to know.

"Trixie." Theo answers.

Dominic and Antonio have a confused look on their faces and I'm sure I do too.

"Who the fuck is, Trixie?" Antonio snaps.

"Why the fuck are you getting other people involved in our business?" Dominic yells. He's pissed.

"Fuck." Theo realizes he hadn't explained to them about Trixie so he goes on to explain all about her. "I didn't, Boss. Two weeks ago, someone hacked into my system. I did everything I could to stop it but coded messages began popping up. When I finally worked out how to access them, I discovered her name."

"Trixie?" Antonio asks.

Theo nods and grips the back of his neck. It's then I see how fucking tired he looks and I wonder if he's had any sleep at all since this whole mess started.

"For the past two weeks, every time I started a search, another coded message would pop up on the screen and I'd have to spend an hour or so unscrambling it." He sighs, I can see his frustration and feel bad for him. "When I entered Bruno J into the search engines, I could only find old articles from years ago. So, I started searching everything on the girls, I started with Darren and it unfolded from there. Trixie started telling me a story and unlocking everything as I went."

"So, you're telling me some woman...." Dominic starts.

"It could be a man." Antonio offers.

"What the fuck, man, woman, I don't give a shit. Someone broke into your failproof system and has led you on a game of cat and mouse? And, this happened after we found Kirsty in the warehouse."

Theo slams his fist onto the table, his own anger escalating. "It's a fucking woman."

"Fuck, Theo. Calm the fuck down." I sound pissed now.

"Everyone can calm the fuck down." Dominic paces the floor. "I want to know everything about this Trixie."

"That's the problem, Boss. I only know what she is prepared to tell me. I can't find shit anywhere and it's pissing me off. I can't figure out how she keeps breaking through our security."

Dominic stops and glares menacingly at Theo. "Are you telling me she has access to everything including our businesses and the shit we're dealing with right now and you don't a fucking thing about her?"

"Si." Theo looks down at his computer. "I think she's trying to help us though, I don't think she's a threat. She could have crippled us by now and she hasn't."

"So, what's the connection with Darren?"

"I don't think there is one."

"So, what the fuck does she want, what is she trying to tell you?" Dominic drags his fingers through his hair.

"It's like building blocks, each piece of information I entered unlocked something different which led me straight to Bruno J. I didn't know it was the same guy, although I suspected it, until Kirsty saw the picture earlier. His name was listed as Byron and you can see the changes he's made. The picture I showed you a couple of weeks ago of Bruno J was taken a few years ago. The one I showed Kirsty is recent, he's had surgery."

"This shit is making my head spin," Antonio growled.

"Theo, keep digging. I want everything on Bruno J, I want to know if he's changed his appearance again now we have Kirsty and I want information on that girl." Dominic sounds a bit calmer now.

"Si, Boss."

"Why do you think she's helping us?" I ask no-one in particular.

Theo answers. "I have a gut feeling she's trying to help. Every time I did a search, she was at her end digging deep and leading me through the right gateways to find information."

"I thought nobody was better than you at this type of thing?" Antonio asks what I've been thinking.

"I think when Miss Katherine's sister went on her rampage she set some sort of wheels in motion which put a firewall in place. It meant no-one could access anything."

"Except this girl?" Dominic asks.

"Si, Boss. I think the only way to access anything beyond that firewall is through this girl. Why the fuck would she be helping us if she's been the one to put it in place?"

We all look at each other, I'm sure we're thinking the same thing. If this girl is helping us, she's also in danger.

I voice my concerns. "Theo, if what you're saying is true, we need to find this Trixie and fast. She could be in danger too if she's caught helping us."

"Fuck." Antonio runs his hand over his face.

Dominic paces the floor again.

When I glance at Theo, the look on his face tells me there is something he hasn't told us. "What is it?"

"I don't know but I have a gut feeling something is wrong. I haven't had a coded message from her since last night and I haven't had time to crack it because I knew you would want to see the information I'd already found first thing this morning."

He returns his attention to the computer and his fingers fly over the keyboard. I saw the flash of fear in his eyes when I mentioned Trixie could be in danger. I think this cat and mouse hunt has just turned into one of survival. It seems Theo has met his match and I heard the admiration in his voice, God help anyone who threatens the life of his little Trixie.

***

The afternoon passes before the girls come back down stairs, I wrap my arms around my girl as soon as she's near. Bending over, I whisper in her ear, "are you okay, Sugar?"

She rests her hands on my arms, leans her head back against my chest and I feel her relax into me.

"I will be." She turns her head to look up at me and I see the shine of tears in her eyes.

I kiss her temple and hold her closer.

Brooklyn urges Evie onto the sofa and puts a movie on the television for her.

Katherine is wrapped in Antonio's arms. I realize how lucky I am to have these people I call family in my life. This shit is far from over but together we'll get through it and for tonight, we can relax and enjoy being together.

"What would you like for dinner?" Brooklyn asks at the same time Dominic's phone sounds.

"Si, Nico." He listens and I watch his expression harden before he speaks again. "We'll be there in ten minutes, tell Demetri to wait there." He listens for another moment. "Call him and tell him I'll be there in ten minutes. Antonio will meet you at the club." He hangs up and everyone remains silent, waiting for him to speak.

"Antonio and I have to leave. Brooklyn, Katherine, I want you both and Evie to stay here where it's safe." "No worries." Kat leans up and kisses Antonio.

Dominic whispers in Brooklyn's ear before kissing her, he then crosses to Evie and crouches down before her. He speaks quietly and she nods.

I walk Dominic and Antonio outside to the cars. "What's going on?"

"Demetri killed a man behind Destiny."

"What the fuck?" Antonio growls.

"I don't know what the fuck happened, all I got was some cazzo attacked a girl in the club. Demetri has taken her to his place because the fucker he killed was part of the Talon MC."

Fuck, now we have a motorcycle gang to deal with on top of everything else.

"Is the girl okay?" I ask.

"Si, as far as I know." Dominic is stressed, he drags his fingers through his hair. "Antonio, go and help Nico clean up the fucking mess at Destiny. I'm going to Demetri's to find out what the fuck is going on."

"What do you need me to do?" I ask.

"Stay here with the girls and Theo, if he finds anything, call me."

"Si Boss." I nod and watch them head to their cars and climb in. After starting the engines, they ease from the driveway.

Fuck can shit get any worse?

Chapter Nineteen

One Week Later

Kirsty

It's been three weeks since Sergio saved me from Hell and a week since I saw the picture of Bruno J on Theo's computer. After spending the day talking with Brooklyn and Katherine, I was determined not to be a scared little girl anymore. Later that night, I headed down to the home gym where Sergio was punching a bag. Instead of standing in the doorway watching, I moved toward him and asked him if he would teach me to fight. He was reluctant at first but I explained, I didn't want to feel weak, I wanted to be able to defend myself if it was needed and he finally agreed.

The first two sessions, he taught me simple moves so if anyone grabbed me I'd be able to get free. After showing me a move and going over and over it for an hour, he'd declare I was tired and send me to bed.

He seemed abrupt, pre-occupied and I became curious after the third session. I waited for him to get in the shower and crept to the door. He was moaning and I wondered if he was hurt but, as I was about to push open the door I heard him grunt and groan my name. I froze in place for a moment before scurrying back up to bed where I pretended to be asleep. He crawled into bed and wrapped me in his arms as if I was the most precious being in the world. It broke my heart and I hurt, knowing I was causing him to suffer because I was scared to let him touch me in that way.

Every night since, for the past week, I've listened to him while he showered and become hot and achy. Last night, I lowered my fingers and touched myself, I was soaking wet just from listening to his moans. I was confused by the way my body was reacting after so much abuse and wasn't sure what I should do. As I'm not allowed to leave the house, I called Brooklyn and asked her to come over so we could have lunch together and chat. Sergio and Theo are hunched over the computer at the dining table, still searching for answers. I've found a recipe book in the kitchen, I've never cooked before but how hard could it be? I place the book on the bench, lean over and flick through the pages until my eyes are drawn to the window and through to the back yard.

"Sugar, what are you doing?" Sergio's deep, honeyed voice never ceases to send shivers of want down my spine.

He wraps his arms around me and I relax into his hold, the warmth of his body seeping through me.

"I'm going to make lunch."

"You were staring through the window; do you want to go and lie in the sun? I can make something for lunch."

"I love how you care for me, Knuckles."

He throws his head back on a deep, full body laugh at the nickname I gave him when he first started training me. I bite my lip, his laughter soothes me, my body tingles. Actually, everything he says and does has this effect on me. I clench my thighs against the ache in my groin.

He holds me tighter and unlike three weeks ago when I would have flinched and pushed him away, I encourage his hold. I accept his touch now, in actual fact, I crave it. He's pressed up against me and if he's noticed me clenching my thighs, he doesn't say anything.

I turn my face up to him. "I want to do it." When his eyes widen, I realize what he thinks I've said. Shit! "I want to cook," I rush out before turning back to the window.

Sergio turns my face toward him and plants a soft kiss on my lips. "Okay, Sugar. If you need help, call out."

I nod my head and he kisses me again before crossing the room back to Theo. I rake my eyes over his body, from head to his sexy ass, I notice he walks with a swagger. The ache intensifies so, I return my attention to the cookbook on the bench and search for something which sounds easy. A quiche recipe leaps out at me, it looks easy enough and sounds delicious. Quiche it is.

***

"Wow that was delicious." Brooklyn sips at her glass of water and rubs a hand over her pregnant belly.

A smile pulls at my lips and I feel proud that I could actually pull it off. "Thank you." I stand, gather the dishes and cross to the sink.

"So, what do you wanna talk about?

I dart my eyes to where Sergio and Theo are engrossed in the computer, shake my head slightly and indicate the back door.

Brooklyn takes my meaning, picks up her glass and follows me outside.

"How do you feel about not having to use a cane anymore?"

121

We sit on the chairs of the outside setting under a large umbrella.

She laughs. "Dominic still treats me like I might break but it feels good being able to move around without having to use a cane to lean on."

"I bet."

"So, enough with the diversion, what's going on?" She sighs, leans back in her chair and takes a mouthful of water. I watch as she places the glass on the table and I stare at the condensation as it runs down the side whilst I fidget with my own glass.

"Kirsty?"

I snap my eyes up to hers and blow out a breath when I see the concern in her eyes.

"I just...." Shit this is harder than I thought. *Just rip off the Band-Aid,* I chant to myself and suck in a deep breath. "I feel achy," I blurt out and lower my head. Fuck, that's not exactly what I meant to say.

"Achy how?" I swear I see panic in her eyes when I look back up.

"Not bad achy." I reassure her. "I mean, down there. I feel achy whenever Sergio is near me." I look her straight in the eyes, hoping she understands.

I watch as she realizes what I'm saying and her eyes widen.

"Do you want him to touch you?" she asks softly.

"I..um...I think I do."

"Then sweety, if you think you're ready, you should talk to Sergio. Tell him how you feel."

"How did you know you were ready after what had happened."

"I'm going to be honest with you. It was different for me. I don't remember the night I was raped, only what he did to me after that." Brooklyn breathes out heavily and closes her eyes.

I feel bad for asking her to relive her past. "I'm sorry, I shouldn't have asked."

"Kirsty, the best thing you can do is talk about what happened to you. If you try to push it away, deny it, it will consume you and you'll never feel free or at peace. The first time Dom touched me, it felt like my body was on fire. I'd never felt anything like it before and knowing he felt the same made it special. I couldn't stop how I felt and even if it had been an option, I wouldn't have. Dom loved me from the first time he laid eyes on me and knowing that made the fall for me worthwhile. When we made love the first time, the Earth shifted, opened up and showed me he was the man I was always meant to be with." Brooklyn has a smile on her face now.

"When Sergio touched you for the first time, how did it make you feel?"

I don't have to think about the answer, it's on the tip of my tongue. "I felt hope and it was like all my nerves had short circuited. When he stopped touching me, I felt an overwhelming sense of loss. I wanted his arms around me, I wanted to be touched, needed it. He made me feel like I was home." I let out a deep breath and gaze up at the bright sun. smiling when a light breeze lifts my hair. God, I love being outside. I jolt at the sudden contact when Brooklyn places her hand over mine and laughs.

"What's so funny?"

"The expression on your face as you relived Sergio's first touch all over again."

"Do you think it's too soon after everything?" It's a question which has played on a loop in my head, a question I haven't been able to answer.

"Do you trust Sergio?"

"With my life." I don't need time to answer that question.

"Then let him help you to feel, to love."

Her words soak into me and I nod. I wonder though, if I have the courage to allow him in. Deep down I know he wants to protect me and he's shown me so much patience and kindness. I know in my very bones, he would never hurt me.

I want to feel. I want to love. I want him to help me.

Chapter Twenty

Sergio

I saunter into the bathroom, strip out of my workout clothes and toss them into the hamper in the corner. I flip the shower taps on cool and step into the huge cubicle. The spray of water pounds into my sore muscles as I lather the soap and wash the sweat from my body.

Once done, I rest my forehead against the tiles and allow the cool water to run down my back. I grip my hard cock and feel it strain against my stomach. I close my eyes and squeeze tight, pumping a few times while picturing Kirsty's small hand working me over instead of mine.

I picture my girl bouncing on her toes and throwing punch after punch into the bag while sweat drips down her face and disappears between her tits. I growl with jealousy now, wishing my tongue had been sucking up every drop. I lick my lips wondering if she'd taste like sweet cinnamon, the scent which fills my nose whenever I'm near her.

"Fuck, I need to get my shit together," I growl before turning, leaning back on the tiles and letting the water run over my chest. I hope in vain it might help soothe my aching cock, nothing else seems to these days.

I grip my rock-hard cock and set a punishing rhythm with my fist. I slam my free hand against the tiles to steady myself when my legs start to shake and I come hard. I grunt as stream after stream hits the tiles and groan Kristy's name. I slump against the tiles when my orgasm is done and suck in deep breaths. When I hear a noise behind me, I swing around and swear I must be fucking dreaming. My spent cock springs back to life as I take in the vision before me. I blink a few times to assure myself I haven't passed out after the force of my orgasm.

Kirsty is real and she's standing in the doorway, she doesn't utter a word but turns and closes the door.

"Sugar...." I groan.

She shakes her head and I close my mouth. I'm not sure what the fuck is happening here and I find myself wanting to give my arm a hard pinch when she begins undressing before me. I lick my lips when she pushes her panties off and anchor my hand against the tiles to stop myself from moving toward her. I try to be a gentleman, I really do but, my eyes have other ideas and they slide over her body. She is fucking gorgeous.

Her long, dark hair hangs over her shoulders and some strands brush her full breasts. I growl when I drop my gaze and see her rosy nipples are hard. My gaze wanders lower and I salivate at the sight of her neatly trimmed pussy.

Fuck, I want a taste of her sweet, sugary scent which surrounds me.

She takes the few steps between us and steps into the shower. A shiver passes through her and I snap out of my haze and switch the water to warm.

I bite down on my lip when she places her soft hands on my chest and runs them up to my shoulders. I feel the slight bite of her nails as she grazes the length of my arms. She grabs my wrists and moves my hands to her waist. I rest them lightly, feeling the warmth of her skin under my fingertips. I let her take things at her own pace, I don't want to scare her.

A growl slips free when she leans forward and peppers kisses over my chest leaving a trail of warmth in their wake. She leans back and her brown doe eyes gaze into mine, I'm not sure what I see there.

"Help me feel, Sergio. Help me to forget," she whispers.

A lump lodges in my throat, I'm not sure what to say.

"Sergio, touch me."

I nod and slide one hand up her back, the other slides over her luscious ass and I give it a gentle squeeze. A soft moan leaves her lips. I find my voice and lean closer to her.

"Are you sure, we don't have to do this?"

I gaze into her eyes before she ducks her head and attempts to step back. I hold her in place and when she looks back up to me, I swear she's on the verge of tears.

"You don't want me, I'm sorry." Her words come out on a sob and it fucking breaks my heart.

"Sugar, you are all I want. I think about you every minute of the day and night but, whether we do this or not, I'm yours." I know she likes it when I tell her I'm hers. I'm careful not to say she's mine because I want her to feel she has control.

"And, I'm yours?" She peers into my eyes.

I nod, surprised by the question, she's never asked me before.

"Say it." She grips my shoulders and I suck in a breath when I hear the strength in her voice.

"I'm yours and you're mine."

"Help me feel, Sergio."

"What do you want me to do, Sugar?"

Surprise that I've asked crosses her face and she runs her hands over me.

"I want..." She blows out a breath, steadying herself. "I want you. Just you. All of you." She stands on tiptoes and runs the tip of her tongue over my lips.

Fuck, it feels like I've waited forever to hear her say those words but, there's something I need to tell her before anything can happen between us.

"I love you, Kirsty."

Her eyes snap to my face and she melts into me. "I love you too, Sergio."

A single tear slides over her cheek, reaching out, I swipe it away.

"Why are you crying? Please don't cry, it hurts me to see you upset."

"No-one has ever said they love me and I've never said it to anyone before."

My fucking heart feels like it's about to shatter in my chest.

"I fucking love you, Sugar." I'll tell her a million fucking times if that's what she needs.

"Kiss me."

Leaning down I take her mouth in a deep kiss and groan at the taste of the sweetest cinnamon as it explodes in my mouth. Gripping her ass in both hands, I lift her into my arms, she wraps her legs around my back. I rest her against the tiles and she arches into me when her back hits the cold tiles. When my hard cock rests against her pussy, she moans and I groan into her mouth. Pulling back, I rest my forehead against hers and wait to catch my breath before speaking.

"We're going to take this slow and if you want to stop you need to tell me."

She nods her head that she understands but it's not enough, I need her words so I squeeze her ass.

"Okay," she breathes out before she leans forward and starts kissing up my neck.

When one of her small hands slides down my chest my muscles jump at the contact and I swear to fuck goosebumps break out across my skin. Her fingers wrap around my hard cock, I lean forward and bury my head into her neck, breathing her in while trying to stop myself from coming all over her hand. Turning her head to the side, I run my tongue over her neck. When she freezes in my arms, I pull back. Fuck.

"I'm sorry, Sugar." I start to put her down but, she tightens her legs around me.

"Don't stop," she begs.

I'm frozen in place, not sure what just happened or what the fuck to do until she grips my cock and starts pumping again.

"Sugar," I warn.

"No, Knuckles, don't stop."

I chuckle at the nickname but it quickly turns into a groan when she swipes the head of my cock against her clit. I lower my head and suck her bottom lip into my mouth causing her to moan out my name. I squeeze my eyes shut as the sound travels straight to my balls, they draw up and I come all over her hand.

"Shit, Sugar."

She doesn't stop stroking me, and I feel my eyes roll back in my head as she milks me until I'm empty. When she rubs the pad of her thumb over the slit, I feel myself getting hard again.

"See what you do to me?" I growl before sucking her earlobe into my mouth.

This time she doesn't freeze but leans closer into me. Sliding my hand around to her stomach, I make my movements slow and deliberate, giving her plenty of time to stop me. I cup one full breast in my hand and run my thumb across the hard point of her nipple.

"Harder," she pants.

"Sugar."

"I'm okay." She leans back against the tiles and locks her eyes on me, I see the plea in her eyes. Spreading my legs a little to brace her, I lift my hands to cup her breasts. I kiss over every scar including the burn mark, determined to help her forget about the past. I settle my mouth over a nipple, wrap my tongue around, suck and nip then repeat on the other. A shiver races through Kirsty and her legs tense around me so I do it again. She whimpers, I claim her lips, kiss her hard, sucking the sounds into my mouth. They are mine, the gentle sounds belong to me and I want them inside me.

Her hand continues to work my cock and when she wriggles higher in my arms, I wonder what she is doing. Then, the head of my cock kisses her pussy. Shivers rage through me like a wildfire. She holds my shoulders and pushes down, reflex has me pushing up against her. She's tight but wet as fuck. I watch her eyes closely as I ease in, groaning as she stretches around me. She arches against me and I hold her close. I ease in until I'm buried balls deep and pause, allowing her to adjust to my size. Tremors from her pussy assault my dick and I growl with satisfaction.

"I need you to move." Her voice is filled with emotion.

I push my hips forward slowly giving her sharp, shallow thrusts but it's not enough for my Sugar and she starts begging for more.

"Sergio, please……"

Her heartfelt plea snaps my control

"Fuck." I piston into her and she bounces on top of me, it's the sexiest fucking sight I've ever seen in my life. "Fucking love you," I moan.

"Love you too." She throws her head back, her milky white neck on display.

Tingles race through me, straight to my balls and they draw up inside me. I can't last much longer. Reaching down, I fondle her swollen clit and within seconds, she tenses, screams out my name and comes all over my cock. It sets off my own release and I erupt inside her, stream after stream, jet after jet of warm cum. I brace myself against the wall of the shower to steady my shaking legs. She clings to me, her head buried in my chest, breathing heavy. I panic, thinking I've hurt her with our frenzied love making.

"Sugar, I'm sorry, did I hurt you?"

It seems to take a huge effort for her to lift her head but, she has a huge smile on her face which accentuates her dimple.

"It was perfect, I love you Sergio." Her tone is sleepy, sated.

Leaning down I kiss her lips softly and breathe into her mouth wanting her to soak my words into her body.

"Tesoro, you are my world, I love you too." I kiss her again and when I pull away, I notice how tired she looks. I wrap my arms around her, turn off the taps – thank fuck for continuous hot water systems, and while I cradle her to my chest, I reach for a towel. Wrapping it over her back, I pad out to our bed.

Chapter Twenty-One

Kirsty

I wake wrapped in Sergio's arms, my head against his warm, hard chest and snuggle closer. I want his touch all over me. I study the tattoos decorating his body and trace my fingers over them one by one, admiring their beauty.

"Morning, Sugar." He runs his hand up and down my back pulling me so close there isn't a sliver of space between us. I love the sound of his voice in the morning, all warm and husky from sleep.

"Morning, Knuckles."

I giggle when a soft growl leaves his lips, I feel so happy when I'm with him. Then, it hits me, since we made love in the shower a few nights ago, I haven't been woken with nightmares. I have actually woken with a smile on my face. Sergio hasn't pushed for sex again, he seems content to just hold me in his arms and I worry he may not have enjoyed it as much as I did. Fuck, I have wanted his touch so badly and even though I built up the courage to be with him, I'm struggling to find it in me again. I want him to reach out to me, to want me, so I won't think he only had sex to please me.

His fingers slide through my hair, I turn my head and kiss his chest, the muscles flinch beneath my lips. I can feel how hard he's become and I wish I had the courage to reach out, wrap my hand around him but, something is holding me back.

"What are you thinking so hard on, Sugar?"

I stay silent, not wanting to put my fears into words, worried about what he might think.

His arms reach around my waist and then I'm straddling his thighs, his hard cock poking at my ass. He reaches up and pushes the hair from my face, tucking it behind my ear. His fingers glide over the shell of my ear and tremors shoot through me from that one simple caress.

"Why haven't you wanted to touch me again?" I duck my head, embarrassed I voiced the words out loud. I allow my hair to fall in front of my face like a shield.

Sergio is not having any of my hiding from him. He lifts my chin using the tips of his fingers, brushes my hair away and when I gaze into his midnight eyes I find them ablaze. It doesn't scare me, warmth seeps through me as I watch hunger take over from the fire.

"Sugar, if you want me to touch you all you have to do is ask."

"Why?" I whisper.

He blows out a deep breath and I worry for a moment that he isn't going to answer.

"I don't want to hurt or frighten you."

"You won't, I trust you." I realize I truly believe what I've said.

Sergio runs his fingers down the side of my face. "Sugar, I stop myself at least a dozen times a day from picking you up, throwing you up against the wall and having my way with you." He pauses and grips my hips to still me, I've been rubbing against him without realizing it.

"Right this minute, I want to throw you on your back and push so deep inside you until you're screaming. But, I can't do it, Sugar." He shakes his head.

I feel the rejection deep inside and move to get out of the bed. I don't want him to see how hurt I am and need to escape. Sergio is having none of it, he grips my thighs and although I know he would let me go if I insisted, I lower myself back onto his hips.

"Sugar…."

I feel anger swell inside and cut him off.

"No. For fuck sake, Sergio. I'm telling you I want to be touched, I want you to fuck me, take me as hard as you want and you're brushing me off. If you don't want to fucking touch me that's fine, leave me be and I'll take care of myself in the shower. You'd know all about doing that." My words are harsh, spat out and his eyes widen. I've never spoken to him this way before but before I can apologize, he flips me onto my back and moves between my legs.

Adrenaline surges through me when he pushes his hard cock around my aching clit. I arch into him and let out a loud moan.

"You want me to fuck you hard, make you scream, make you moan?" Sergio growls at me.

135

I nod.

"You want me to prove to you that I'm yours and your mine? That I care about you?"

His rough hand slides over my thigh, he grips my panties and with one tug, they're gone. My voice has left me, I can't form words. I raise my feet and using my heels, I push the shorts from his body. The head of his cock hits my pussy and he groans.

I slept in one of his shirts last night and he tears it open, buttons ping off in all directions. His mouth dives on my hard nipple at the same time his cock slides through the lips of my pussy. I groan, my breath comes in short pants and I call his name over and over.

"Please…" I choke out.

He thrusts deep, his hands are all over me and he increases the depth and speed of his thrusts. My nails scrape at his back and Sergio hisses and holds me closer.

"Is this what you want?" he growls.

"Yesss," I hiss, my body is on fire.

"Fuck, your pussy is gripping me so hard, Sugar. Your muscles are so tight."

Sergio slides his hands under my thighs, lifts my hips and pistons into me. My eyes roll back in my head, I tense and teeter on the edge of a hard orgasm.

"Come now, Sugar," he demands and I crash over the edge with a scream.

I'm floating when I feel him release inside me and it sets off another orgasm. I grip his shoulders; my nails pressing into his skin and ride the waves of pleasure. As we both struggle for breath, I open my eyes to see sheer panic in Sergio's eyes.

"What's wrong?"

"Fuck, Sugar. I'm so sorry." He closes his eyes and takes deep breaths.

"Why are you sorry?"

"I was too rough with you."

Well that just pisses me off. "Sergio, don't you dare ruin it. What we did was amazing, I've never felt anything like it." I take a deep breath and confess a truth I have been holding back when I see the uncertainty in his eyes. "I want you to take control of my body. I want to know you want me and you aren't afraid to take what you want. I know you think after everything I have been through I can't handle it but, I can, I'm not made of fucking glass. And, I know if I said stop, you would. I trust you, Sergio."

"Fuck. I love you, Sugar." Leaning forward, he takes my lips in a bruising kiss which makes my toes curl. I feel his dick flex inside me as it hardens and I moan as he starts a slower pace this time. Easing back, I squeeze my inner muscles around him and he groans loudly.

"Again, Sugar?"

I nod, he picks me up and I wrap my legs around his waist. He stays inside me as he carries me to the ensuite.

"Shower. I want to get you all clean while I make you dirty."

I laugh at his way of thinking and lean in for a kiss. I can feel myself glowing. I'm feeling very loved up right now.

"I love you." I lean back in his arms and see so much love in his eyes. For the first time in my life, I know what it feels like to be loved.

Chapter Twenty-Two

Sergio

I leave Kirsty to dress, throw on shorts and a singlet and head downstairs to the kitchen. My Sugars moans as I took her hard against the shower wall are still clear in my mind. I can feel the marks her nails left on my back and I feel a sense of pride that she branded me as hers.

I pad across the kitchen to the fridge and pull out the bacon and a carton of eggs. I'm eager to have breakfast ready for when she comes down, I'm sure she must be hungry because I'm fucking starving after our workout. But, not only for food, I crave the flavor of her on my lips in my mouth. I swear to Christ, she takes like sweet cinnamon.

A throat being cleared behind me draws my attention. I swing around to find Theo seated at the table and I growl, pissed off. He probably heard my girl's screams of passion and those are for me, nobody else. He obviously sees my irritation and he holds up his hand.

"I just walked in the door but, I'm guessing you and Kirsty were...."

I cut him off with a growl and fuck me, he chuckles.

"Settle down big fella, the scratch marks on your shoulders are a dead giveaway."

I smile and shake my head, the irritation disappearing.

"Found anything?" I nod my head to the computer in front of him.

"Yeah, it's why I'm here so early."

Before I can ask him what it is, my phone rings. I cross to the breakfast bar and when I pick it up, Dominic's name flashes on the screen. I hit the answer button and speak.

"Boss, Theo is here, he found......."

Dominic cuts me off. "Sergio, some cazzo set fire to Destiny, I need you to meet me there."

"Fuck," I growl angrily and run a hand over my face.

I won't refuse him, he hasn't asked me to do shit except look after Kirsty and keep at Theo for the past month.

"Si, Boss, give me twenty minutes and I'll meet you. Do we know who it was?"

"Si, I think it has to do with Demetri's Butterfly."

"Demetri's what?" I ask as I head for the stairs.

"I'll explain more when you get here. Make sure Theo keeps his eyes on Kirsty. Mickey is on his way to keep watch out the front."

"Si, Boss."

He ends the call and I hurry up the stairs to get ready and to let Kirsty know I have to go out.

***

When I pull the car up to the front of Destiny and scan the area I note the front doesn't look too badly damaged. I step from the car, lock it and head around the side of the building where I find Dominic, Antonio and Nico.

"Boss." I give the men a chin lift and note the damage to the back of the building.

"About fucking time, Sergio."

Anger wells in me at Dominic's words but I don't let it get the better of me. I know he's stressed about everything and now isn't the time to say shit so I keep my mouth shut.

"How's Kirsty?" Antonio asks.

"Better." He chuckles when I smile.

My eyes turn back to Dominic as he storms past me. "We need to get a handle on this shit."

"Why do you think it has something to do with the woman Demetri has?" I ask.

Dominic doesn't say a word. We follow him as he walks around a corner to the back of the building where there's a small maintenance shed, a symbol for the motorcycle club has been sprayed on the front in red paint.

"Fanculo!" I spit.

Dominic turns to face us and points at me. "You and me are going to see Demetri while Antonio and Nico clean up this fucking mess." Anger rolls off him in waves.

I nod and turn to head back to the car. Dominic follows, he shouts something over his shoulder to Antonio but doesn't stop walking. I slide into the driver's seat of my car and Dominic climbs in beside me. I start the car and ease onto the road while he tells me about the girl Dimitri is helping.

"The girl's name is Sophie and she was the old lady of a guy called Ace."

"The cazzo Demetri shot?"

"Si, from what I hear he was a nasty fucker. My heart doesn't bleed for a fucker like that but by killing him, we have brought the MC down on us."

He blows out a deep breath and I take my eyes off the road for a second to glance at him. He looks more stressed than I've ever seen him. Fuck, so much has happened in the past couple of months including shit with Bruno J and Paulie DeMarko.

"You said on the phone, Theo found something?" He taps his fingers on the armrest on the door.

"Si, but I left before he could tell me."

"Shit, okay. Once we figure out what's happening with Demetri, we'll head to your place and find out. Does Kirsty know the *safe house* is your place?"

My stomach twists knowing I have been keeping it from her but, it's never really come up in our conversations. I shake my head as we pull up at Demetri's.

"Sergio, she needs to be told."

"Si, I know, Boss."

We get out of the car and cross to the electric gate in the fence which surrounds Demetri's home. Dom punches in the code and we wait while the gate opens.

I look up to see Demetri waiting for us on the porch.

"Boss, Sergio," he greets.

"Ciao, Brother," I answer.

"We need to talk." Demetri nods to Dominic and leads us inside to the kitchen.

I stop short at the sight of a beautiful girl dressed in Demetri's clothes. She has long mousy brown hair and piercing green eyes. She's tall but not as tall as us and she has nice curves. There is fear in her eyes and the bruises on her face are only now fading.

"Butterfly, can you give us a minute?" Dimitri smiles.

She nods, picks up her coffee and heads for the back door. We watch as she leaves and when we hear the back door close, Demetri speaks.

"What happened?"

Dominic explains about the fire at the club and the spray paint. Demetri runs his hand over his bald head.

"Boss, I'm sorry I did that shit at the club but I'm not sorry I killed him." He breaths out heavily. "He lorded it over everyone in the club that night and then gripped my girl so hard, she squealed and flinched in pain. He dragged her from the club to the alley out back where he wanted to fucking rape her. She fought him hard but he punched her in the face." He slams his hands down on the kitchen bench, lowers his head, sucks in a deep breath before looking back up and continues. "I'm glad that fucker is dead and I'd kill him again in a heartbeat if he was here now."

"Fuck, Demetri, I wasn't pissed you killed the fucker. I'm pissed it happened where it did." Dom means we don't draw attention to ourselves, we take that shit to the docks, out of sight.

I replay Demetri's words in my head and ask, "your girl?"

"Si, I knew she was my girl the minute she walked into the club. The things that fucker did to her, he's lucky I shot him and he died fast." He paces the floor. "What now?"

"You keep your ass here with that girl and leave the rest to us. We need to settle this shit. I'll get Antonio to call you."

"Si, Boss." He flips the kettle on at the same time we here the back door open.

When I turn, his girl is standing looking at all of us.

"Butterfly, this is Dominic and Sergio. This is Sophie." Demetri introduces us all and she slowly makes her way over to shake our hands. She's pretty but my girl is all I need.

"Let's have a coffee," Demetri says.

I want to say no, that I have to get back to my girl but, Dominic beats me to it.

"We have some other stuff to take care of but bring Sophie over to the house sometime this week. Once Brooklyn learns of her, she'll aggravate the shit out of me until they meet."

Demetri and I chuckle. There isn't a man alive who would risk annoying Dominic, not if they wanted to keep their teeth but, Brooklyn could ask anything of him and he'd fall to his knees to make sure she's happy.

We leave the house, get back into the car and head back to my place ten minutes away. I remain silent as I drive, I know not to speak when Dom is deep in thought. I pull into my driveway and switch off the engine.

"Let's find out what Theo found, have a coffee and I'll take you back to your place."

"Si, brother."

We stride to the door, I twist the handle and push it open. I'm frozen in place when I see my place has been tossed. I shout out for Kirsty but there's no answer, I know in my gut she's not here but I bolt up the stairs with my heart in my throat. I search the rooms frantically but there's nothing.

"Fuck," Dominic yells and a string of Italian curse words follow.

I barrel back down the steps, taking them two at a time and race to the kitchen. Theo is on the floor, his laptop smashed into pieces beside him but that's not what has my blood running cold.

Dominic is standing in front of someone and there is blood everywhere. I'm too scared to step aside to see who it is. Dominic steps away and I see Mickey strapped into a chair, he's dead. He's been fucking tortured.

Dominic snatches a paper from Mickey's chest and reads what it says.

"Fucking piece of shit!" He screams out before kicking a small table across the room.

I take the paper from his hands and every muscle in my body locks up, I'm ready to kill after I see the words which are written....

Can't save her now

Chapter Twenty-Three

Kirsty

"Wake up, you stupid little bitch."

I groan in pain when someone kicks me hard in the stomach. I roll over, coughing hard, feeling like I'm going to throw up. When I blink my eyes open, I see Bruno J standing above me. Tears flood my eyes when I remember what had happened earlier.

"You honestly thought you could get away from me little pie? You thought those assholes could protect you?" He bends forward and cackles in my face, my stomach rolls at the stench of his breath. I can't believe I'm back here, I'd tried to fight them but there were too many of them and when I saw what they'd done to Theo, I gave up.

I sob when I think about what they'd done to Mickey, strapping him to a chair. His screams echoed in the house, they were questioning him and when he refused to

147

answer, they would cut him. I begged him to tell them what they wanted to know, but no matter what they did, he stayed firm and I was forced to watch as the life drained from his eyes.

"Time to get up." Bruno J grabs a handful of my hair and drags me onto my feet.

Instinctively, my hands flew to my head to lessen the pain. With his free hand, he slaps me hard across the face, splitting my lip. I run my tongue along the stinging wound and taste blood in my mouth.

He drags me to the wall and pushed me into place by jamming his shoulder into my chest, knocking the air from my lungs. He snaps handcuffs, hanging from a ring on the wall, to my wrists. I suck in my breath when he pulls out a knife and slices it through my clothes, leaving me in only bra and panties.

"Okay little pie, it's time to teach you all over again. To teach you all the lessons you knew before those fucking Italians took you." He shakes his head. "I have a friend I owe you to and it's cost me a fucking fortune to hold him off until I could get you to him. So, you're going to repay me by being a good girl and doing exactly as you're told. Aren't you?" He grabs my face hard and I wince at the pain in my lip before nodding. I close my eyes willing Sergio to find me. A tear slides free, I know what is coming.

Bruno J leans forward and rams his tongue into my mouth, instead of giving up and accepting my fate, I latch on with my teeth and bite down as hard as I can. I taste his blood in my mouth.

He yells, pulls back and curses as his arm draws back and he punches me hard in the face. Because I'm bound against the wall, I have no way to avoid it and take the full force.

"You stupid little bitch." He spits blood onto the floor by my feet. "Karen!" he screams out. I hear the sound of high heels clicking on the tiled floor. I cringe inwardly, trying not to let my fear show.

"Pie needs another lesson before Paulie gets here. Don't mark her up too bad or he won't take her."

"Sure thing, Boss." She has a sadistic smile on her face and I brace for what's to come next. I close my eyes when I hear the door close and her cheap perfume surrounds me.

I close my eyes and calm my racing heart by thinking about what Sergio had said. *I am yours and you are mine.* I'm stronger than I was because of him, because of his love. I need to fight for me. For us. To feel. I hear a cupboard door close and when I hear the crack of a belt, I open my eyes. I watch as she stalks toward me.

"I told you, you can never hide from us." She cackles viciously.

The first couple of blows land and I suck in a breath against the pain. I become lax, allowing the cuffs to take my weight, my head lowered. I lift my eyes and watch her return to a cupboard, she puts the belt away before coming back to me. I take deep breaths, my legs sting and shake.

Karen reaches up and unfastens the handcuffs and I realize this is my only chance. I blow out a deep breath, steadying myself as both arms are released.

I grab the bitch's shoulders. Lean back and head butt her. My head spins at the hard contact but I steady myself, I look up to see her holding her nose which pours blood.

149

"You stupid little bitch," she screams. Before she can make a move, I punch her in the face. Left. Right. Left. Exactly as Serio taught me. She lands on her ass on the floor and one of her shoes slides free. I snatch it up. I'm not thinking when I jump on her and start hitting her in the face with the heel, my final swing punctures her eye and blood spurts all over us both.

I push away, scurrying along the floor on my ass, watching as she collapses into a pool of her blood. I take a deep breath and smile when I think of how proud Sergio would be. When a door slams open, I jump to my feet, ready to fight again.

Chapter Twenty-Four

Sergio

"Make sure Nico stays with them until I get back and get him to make sure the alarms are on." Dominic paces as he speaks into his phone. "Si, now get your ass here." He ends the call and jams the phone in his pocket.

"Boss, I need to go and find her." I sound pissed because I am. We're wasting time and thinking about what could be happening to my woman is driving me out of my mind. I hear Theo groan and turn to see him sitting on the sofa.

"Fucken assholes," he spits out while rubbing the side of his head.

"The bullet grazed the side of your head, I stitched you up. You'll be fine but you'll probably have a headache for a while." Doc packs up his bag.

151

I slam a bottle of pain tablets down on the table in front of him along with a glass of water.

"Talk." I fold my arms across my chest. I know I'm being an asshole right now but I need the information.

"Fuck, Sergio, give him a second," Dominic growls.

"We don't have a fucking second!" I shout out in frustration. I feel the weight of Dom's hand come down on my shoulder and he gives it a squeeze. Uncrossing my arms, I run a hand through my hair, trying to calm down.

"I need my laptop." Theo slams his glass down on the table after taking a couple of pills.

"It's smashed to fucking pieces," I inform him.

"I have a spare in the car."

Thank fuck. I race out to his car and thank fuck it's unlocked. I reach inside and push the button to release the boot, grab the laptop and head back inside to where Theo is now waiting at the kitchen table. I place it down and wait for what feels like forever for him to start it up. He taps the keyboard and when he swings it toward us, there's another picture of Bruno J on the screen. This one is different though, there's a woman with him.

"When I was searching through everything last night this picture popped up. Her name is Karen." He points to the picture of the brown-haired woman.

"I dug a little deeper and it turns out she's indebted to Bruno J. She lives in Stockton. She also has a place in Sydney but my bet is they are in Stockton at the moment and that's where Kirsty is."

"Let's go," Dominic orders at the same time Antonio races through the door. He looks different and it takes me a few seconds to realize his arm is no longer in a sling.

"What's up with that?" I point at his arm.

"Fuck, I was over it, I don't need it."

I nod before we race to one of the cars out front and jump in. I hope to Christ we get to my woman in time.

***

We crawl down the street until we come to an old run-down house, fuck, it's barely standing and calling it a house is a bit of a stretch. It's taken us twenty-five minutes to get here and my stomach is churning, thinking what they could be doing to my girl. I don't blame Antonio, there was no faster way to get here. There's only one bridge which leads into Stockton and it's busy as shit because the road over runs through an industrial area.

We pull to a stop a couple of doors up and Antonio switches off the engine. "How are we going to do this, Boss?" He checks his guns and I pull mine out again, ready to get this shit over and done with.

"Sergio and I will go through the front door, you cover the back and catch anyone who tries to escape. It's time we ended this shit, here and now."

"What the fuck are we hanging around for?" I growl before stepping out of the car.

Dominic grabs my arm. "Sergio, calm down and get your shit together or instead of getting your woman, you'll leave the house in a body bag."

"Clear heads," Antonio says as he joins us.

I know what they say is true but I'm struggling to control myself. I need my woman back in my arms, to know she's safe. I nod at the pair of them even though I'm churning with worry.

We make quick work of crossing the front yard to the front of the house and Antonio keeps to the shadows as he creeps around back.

I peek through the torn curtains at the front window and see two men talking. I look back to Dom and hold up two fingers. When I look back, I see another person come from downstairs and head towards the back. I turn back to Dom and indicate one more. He nods his understanding.

We creep to the front door and Dominic gives a signal before smashing in the front door. The old wood offers no resistance and it splinters on impact before what's left crashes against a wall. We barge in and start shooting.

BANG!

BANG!

The odor of nitroglycerin, sawdust, and graphite swirls in the air and bullet shells drop to the floor with a metallic ping.

The two men in the front room drop to the floor. Dead. I swing around and point my gun toward the other man who has swung towards us. It's fucking Bruno J. His hand moves to the back waistband of his pants but before he can reach for a gun, Antonio explodes through the back door and pushes his gun to Bruno J's head.

"Nice and easy." Antonio's tone is menacing.

Bruno J moves his hand slowly and drops his gun to the floor. Antonio kicks it away.

I cross the floor and get up in the asshole's face. "Where the fuck is she?"

"Fuck you," he spits.

I aim my gun to his leg and shoot out his kneecap. He drops to the floor screaming in pain.

"Where is she?"

"Fucken piece of shit, I own her not you!"

This asshole has a death wish. I aim my gun at his other knee but before I can shoot he gets to his feet and raises his arm. Antonio grabs it and shoots him through the palm. He falls back to the floor screaming in pain and I watch as blood pools around him.

"One more time you piece of shit, where the fuck is she?"

"Downstairs!" he screams when Antonio jams his foot on the hand which was shot.

I take off at a dead run and take the stairs two at a time until I reach the bottom. I notice what looks like cellar doors and wonder why everything down here has been sound proofed. I dash to the only closed door, flip all the locks and slam the door open.

Pride wells within me when I see her in a fighting stance, ready to take me on. The woman in the picture with Bruno J is lying on the floor, blood surrounds her. I do a double take, fuck, is that a high heel shoe sticking out of her eye? I shake my head and move into the room slowly, giving Sugar time to see it's me.

"Sugar, baby," I whisper.

I watch as her face crumples and she runs straight into my open arms.

"You came," she sobs into my neck.

"Always, Tesoro mio." I wrap my arms tight around her and feel her flinch. I pull back and when I look, I see fresh bruises appearing over her stomach. Fucken piece of shit.

"I'm so sorry, Sugar."

"I'm fine now you're here." She leans in and kisses me.

"Come on, let's get you home."

She wraps her arms around me and holds on as I carry her back upstairs. When we enter the kitchen, I see Antonio and Dominic have tied Bruno J to a chair. Dominic is standing in front of him with a knife. Kirsty wriggles against me and when I look into her eyes, she's pleading with me.

"What is it, Sugar?"

"There's something I need to do."

I slide her down my body until her feet touch the floor and remember she is in a ripped shirt with only her bra and panties on. I slip my shirt off, remove the torn one from her and replace it with mine. Slowly she turns and takes a few steps towards Bruno J.

"Little pie," he gasps.

The nickname grates down my spine. "What the fuck you call her?" Dominic pushes the knife to his throat.

"You don't fucking speak to her!" Antonio grabs a handful of hair and rips his head back.

Kirsty crosses to the drawers and is rummaging in them. I wondering what she's doing until she turns with something shiny in her hands. She pushes back her shoulders and steps in front of Bruno J, I watch as his eyes widen and when I glance at her hands, I see the ice pick she is holding.

She leans forward and I growl when she speaks to him. She is too fucking close to the piece of shit. I look at Antonio when he chuckles and then hear Bruno J scream out like a little bitch.

Kirsty stabs the asshole in the balls with the ice pick and it has us all wincing. She lifts her arm and repeatedly stabs at his sac, he screams in agony. She spits in his face, drops the ice pick and turns back to me. I open my arms and she moves into them.

I knew she needed to do what she did, but fuck I hated my woman being so close to him.

"Sergio, take Kirsty to the car while we finish him off."

"Si, Boss."

I lift Kirsty into my arms and as I turn to leave, I stiffen at Bruno J's words.

"Paulie is still com…," he coughs. "….coming for you."

The words hang in the air as Dominic slices his throat.

"We need to get back, I found something Theo is going to want to know," Dominic says.

"What fucking now?" Antonio asks.

I don't hear anymore as I cradle my girl close to my chest and head for the car.

Chapter Twenty-Five

Kirsty

I wrap my arms around Sergio and hold on tight, not wanting to let go. I breathe in his scent as he carries me to the car and plant a light kiss to his neck, I feel his pulse point jump at the contact.

"Sugar, I need to take care of you right now." He leans down and kisses my forehead. I feel so precious when he does things like that.

"I love you." A lump forms in my throat when I think about how I never thought I would get the chance to tell him again.

Sergio stops when we reach the car and he gazes down into my eyes. They are so full of deep heat mixed with love that my body begins to hum.

"I love you too, Sugar." He blows out a breath, leans his forehead against mine and places his hand against my cheek. "I was so fucking scared when I found you were gone. I haven't felt that way for a long time."

I run my fingers over the five o'clock shadow on his jaw and wonder why he was scared before. This man doesn't strike me as someone who scares easily, we all have pasts I guess.

"Will you tell me one day?" I realize he may not know what I mean. "About your past." I squeeze his hand which has Marcella tattooed on it, hoping he gets my meaning.

"Si, Sugar, I will tell you but not right now."

"Okay, Nocche."

He sucks in a deep breath when I call him knuckles in Italian. I'd asked Theo this morning about it. I gasp when visions of Theo being shot and Mickey being tortured enter my mind. I didn't know Mickey very well but he was trying to protect me and it tears me apart knowing he paid for it with his life.

"What's wrong, Sugar?" I hadn't realized I was crying until Sergio wipes the tears from me eyes.

"How's Theo, is he alive? I'm so sorry about Mickey."

"Doc says Theo will be okay and Mickey..... He was like a brother to me and it hurts like fuck that he's dead but, knowing he gave his life trying to protect you means he will always have a special place in my heart.

I can see Sergio's eyes are glassy with tears and I hug him tighter. He rests the top of his head on mine. After a moment, he opens the car door and climbs in while still holding me.

When I glance through the window, I see Dominic and Antonio heading our way. Dom is holding a bag and I wonder what he has in it.

They cross the road but when they reach the car, they don't get inside. Instead, they go to the boot and within minutes, they head back across the road. I notice a tin can in Antonio's hand and wonder what they're doing.

Sergio rubs my back while I peer out the window. I turn find he's watching too and a smile curls his lips. When I turn back to the window, the men are headed back to us. Behind them, I see smoke rising from what was my own private Hell. The fire catches hold and I feel lighter knowing no-one will ever have to set foot in the place again.

Antonio climbs into the driver's seat and starts the engine while Dom slides in beside him. As we drive away, I take one last look at the house. Flames are shooting up and black smoke hangs in the air. I turn back and snuggle deeper into Sergio's hold.

Dom turns to look at us from the front seat. "We'll head to my place. Theo is there and I know Brooklyn will want to see Kirsty is okay."

"Are you okay with that, Sugar?" Sergio whispers in my ear and it vibrates to my core.

I would love to have a shower but I have a feeling Dominic needs Sergio so I nod. I'm okay as long as I'm not alone right now.

"Si, Boss." Sergio answers as he wraps his arms around me a little tighter.

A phone rings and Antonio answers. "Si, Kitten, we have her……okay, see you soon." He pauses and chuckles. "Okay, love you too."

160

"Kat is meeting us at your place, Boss," he tells Dom.

"Bene. What was so funny?"

"She said to tell you it's lucky we found Kirsty or she would have kicked our asses."

I smile when I feel Sergio's deep chuckle.

"Fuck, when did our women start thinking they were in charge?" Dom growls but it's obvious he's not angry. It's more like he's confused about how the tables have turned.

"Boss, the minute we laid eyes on them." Antonio laughs.

Sergio kisses the top of my head and I giggle, he's in the same boat.

"See, we are all fucking pussy whipped." Dominic's statement causes everyone in the car to burst into laughter.

God it feels good to fucking laugh. My man's arms feel so good around me, I can't wait to be alone with him again. You would think, after everything that's happened that I would want to keep everyone at arm's length. Push them away. But, this man has done so much to help me. He's made me feel again. He's given me hope that my life can be normal and most of all, he showed me I can be strong and stand up for myself.

Chapter Twenty-Six

Sergio

Antonio eases the car into Dominic's long driveway and I pull my girl closer into my chest as I watch the high gates swing open. I love how her body melts into mine. I look up when I hear Dominic cursing and scan the area.

"Who the fuck is that?" Dominic opens the car door and leaps out before the car comes to a stop.

"Sergio, take Kirsty to the guest house." Antonio shouts before switching off the car. He jumps out and I see his gun is drawn as he chases after the Boss who is now at one side of the front door with his gun also drawn.

When I look closely, I see what has Dominic so wired. Theo and Kat's cars are in the driveway but, behind Kat's is a black SUV with blacked out windows. Brooklyn and Evie will be in the house and Nico should be too. Fuck, something's wrong.

I don't want to take a risk and endanger Kirsty so I place my fingers on her lips, asking her to stay quiet and quickly get out of the car. With her in my arms, I race for the guest house. I push the door open and stand off to one side, doing a quick sweep of what I can see. I can't see or hear anyone so I lower Kirsty to her feet. Reaching down, I pull a small hand gun from under the leg of my jeans and hand it to her. She grips it hard, holding it close to her chest.

Quietly I lead her inside to the sofa in the living room and turn her to face the doorway. "Stay here, Sugar. I need to check out the rest of the house. If anyone comes near you, point and shoot. The gun is loaded and ready." I do a quick sweep of the guest house and when satisfied, I head back to Kirsty. "No-one's here, I'm going over to the house to see what's going on. Lock the door after me and don't come out."

She reaches out and her fingertips brush over my still naked chest, I look into her eyes and see she doesn't want me to leave her. "I have to make sure they're okay." She nods. I don't want to leave her but I have to. I lean over and brush her lips with mine.

"Be careful, Sergio."

I nod and head through the door, I hear the lock click as I move away. I'll be worried as fuck until I get back to her but I have to make sure no-one in the house is in danger. I creep up to the glass doors at the back of the house and peek in from the side, taking stock of the situation before me.

A man is holding Brooklyn with a knife at her pregnant belly, Katherine is on the ground and isn't moving. Fuck! Dominic, Antonio, Nico and Theo all have their guns aimed at the man. I can see by the way the muscles in Dom's neck are corded that it's taking every ounce of control to stay where he is. I push on the door and it opens slightly, I can now hear what is being said.

"Release the woman," Dominic demands.

I do a quick sweep and see there are five men. Easy enough to take down if the women weren't in the house.

"I won't fucking say it again, release the woman."

I hear groaning and Antonio calls out. "Katherine, open your eyes, baby."

Fuck. If I storm in and start shooting, shit could get ugly real fast. I need to think. I need a way for us to get out of this safely. When I hear *his* voice, I freeze. Paulie DeMarko!

"You have such good taste, Mr. Grasso, such pretty women. It would be a shame if something was to happen to her." He runs his hand down her face.

"Don't fucking touch me," Brooklyn shouts.

"Touch her again and I will personally pull out every one of your teeth before I slit your throat." Dominic is becoming impatient with the situation.

Paulie laughs and images of Marcella crash into my mind. Beaten, bloodied, Paulie standing over her with a gun aimed at her head. She was my sister and I couldn't protect her but I won't fail Kristy, he'll be dead before he gets the chance to lay a fucking hand on her.

I look down at my chest, the scars a reminder of the last time we crossed paths, when I tried to rescue my sister from him. I was younger then, smaller, not as strong as I am now. Dominic had found me lying in a pool of blood, took me back to his place and had me stitched up. He saved my

164

life and I have been by his side ever since, I will not fail him now. I step through the door and raise my gun in line with his head.

"Don't. Fucking. Touch. Her. Asshole!"

He swings around to face me and laughs like the lunatic he is. "Let me tell you how it's going to be. You have something of mine and I think I have someone who may mean something to one of you." He glares at us but it's Theo who speaks in a whisper.

"Trixie."

Paulie faces Theo and clucks his tongue. "You're a smart one. You give me my little pie and I will give you Trixie. If you don't, I'll kill Trixie and have her body dumped on your doorstep."

A trade, he wants a fucking trade! I glance at Theo wondering if he's tempted but he shakes his head.

Then, I hear a loud bang from behind me and all hell breaks loose. Bullets start flying and I swing around to find my brave Sugar with the gun in her hand and an angry look on her face.

Dominic yells for the girls to get down and they drop to the floor, except Kirsty. I back toward her and hold her behind me. There is no way Paulie is going to get his fucking hands on her.

Bullets ricochet around the room, time passes in a blur of smoke before the shooting finally comes to an end. I swing around and pull Kirsty into my chest, thank fuck she's in one piece. I turn to make sure the others are okay.

"Dominic, you need to find Evie," Brooklyn screams from where she is on the floor and he sprints away.

Kat's eyes are open and she's sitting up, Antonio is checking her for injuries.

"How the fuck did they get in here, the Boss said to make sure the place was fucking secured?" Antonio snarls at Theo.

"It's not their fault, Antonio, they followed me through the gate before it had a chance to close," Kat explains.

Nico bursts back inside, he had chased after one of the men. "He got away. The fucker got away."

"Who?" I ask but I already know who it was.

"The asshole who was in charge of these goons."

"Paulie DeMarko." Kirsty stiffens in my arms when I say his name.

"He's going to fucking die," Dominic yells as he comes toward us. He's carrying a crying, shaking, very frightened Evie in his arms. She holds her arms out to Brooklyn after Nico helps her to stand.

Brooklyn moves closer and the little girl flings herself at her mother. "Mummy."

Once Evie is in his fiancé's arms, Dominic surrounds them in his arms and hugs them to him before kissing Brooklyn's forehead. When he releases them, he begins to pace the floor like a caged lion.

"He tied my daughter to her fucking bed!"

"Fanculo."

"Piece of shit."

"That cazzo is fucking dead."

The anger in all of us is palpable.

"Angel pack a bag now," Dominic snaps.

Brooklyn nods and repositions Evie in her arms but being heavily pregnant she's struggling.

Kat gets to her feet after reassuring Antonio she's fine and sweeps Evie into her arms. Kirsty wiggles in my arms and I let her go.

We watch as the girls head upstairs to help Brooklyn do as Dominic said.

Blood is pumping hard in my veins, I want….no, need to kill the motherfucker. My eyes look to the three of his men who now lie dead on the floor.

"Nico, I want you at Sergio's to update security. Theo, you go too, set your shit up and find something on DeMarko and your girl. We'll talk more about your girl later."

Nico and Theo nod and head for the door.

Dominic continues firing off instructions. "Antonio call some of the men from Sydney and get them up here, we're going to need their help, we're about to face a fucking shit storm. Contact Frankie and find out if he's settled things with the Chinese, we need to start ticking this shit off." Dom runs fingers through his hair and I see the frustration on his face. "Sergio, call Demetri and let him know a war is coming, tell him to keep a close eye on Sophie as we still have that shit coming our way too. Destiny is closed for repairs so he has no reason to be apart from her right now. We'll all head to your place."

I nod, pull the phone from my pocket and hit Demetri's number. Fuck, war is coming and we need to get shit locked down fast because if anything happens to any of our women, the son of a bitch who harms one hair on their heads is already dead.

Chapter Twenty-Seven

Kirsty

As Sergio makes his way upstairs, I snuggle closer in his arms. I told him I was fine to walk up on my own but he didn't listen. He just grunted and refused to put me down. What's the point in arguing, if it makes him happy then I'll go along with it? I'm fricken exhausted so it's easier to let him have his own way. Everyone is heading for the kitchen or the bedrooms which Sergio showed them when we first arrived. I really wanted to stay downstairs but I also want to shower, to wash away the filth of the day and the feel of Bruno J's hands.

Sergio doesn't stop when we enter our bedroom, he takes me straight through to the bathroom and places me onto the bench with the double sinks, my back is against the mirror mounted onto the wall. He plants his hands on each side of my hips, drops his head and takes a deep breath. His muscles flex and I feel a cool drop hit my bare thigh. I reach out and lift his head with my palms. Tears stream from his eyes and my heart squeezes at the sight. I bring his head to my chest, his hands wrap around my waist and my nipples harden when his hot breath washes over me. I ignore my want and caress his back with my hands.

"Talk to me, Sergio," I whisper. I know something is terribly wrong.

"I need you right now." He trails warm kisses up my neck and I hum with approval.

I'm well aware that we can be noisy and we're not alone so I hit a button on the wall which I discovered the other day and music floats from speakers. It's *Breathe* by *Faith Hill*. I had the song on repeat after I found it, I'm addicted to it. It's perfect for now.

I feather my fingertips over Sergio's back, he moves up and hovers over my lips. But, he doesn't kiss me. I lick my lips in anticipation but he's standing there, staring.

"We don't have to do this if you need time."

I see the uncertainty in his eyes and I know he's concerned but I need this, I need all of him to wash away everything.

"I need you, Knuckles." I flick the tip of my tongue over his lips and he groans before crashing his mouth against mine.

I moan with desire when his tongue slides in, tasting my mouth. He slides the shirt from my shoulders and the rough of his palms causes goosebumps to break out over my skin. With the shirt gone, he makes quick work of my bra and panties. Wrapping my legs around his waist, I pull him back to me, his mouth back to mine.

Gripping my ass in both hands, he rubs his hard cock against me and I arch into him, wanting him in me. His lips latch onto a hard nipple and I hold him there, running my fingers through his thick hair. I love the feel of him plucking and nipping at my aching breast.

"Need you now." I'm breathless with want.

He releases the nipple and kisses the other one before unzipping his pants. I slide my hand over the ridges and valleys of his six pack and under the waistband of his briefs. I palm his hard cock and stroke up and down.

Pushing him back, I note the confusion on his face as I slide from the bench and onto my knees. I kneel before him, knowing what I want. I slide his briefs to his ankles, hold his length in my hand and as my mouth closes around him, I gaze into his eyes. He's far too big for me and my mouth has to stretch around him. I lap at the tip, sliding my tongue over the slit which causes his moans and groans to echo around us.

Blowing out a deep breath, I suck his length until it hits the back of my throat. Ignoring the gag reflex, I relax my muscles and take him all the way in. My eyes water slightly but when I look up into his midnight eyes and watch them roll with ecstasy, it's all worth it.

His hands are on the back of my head, his fingers wrapped in my hair. I wait for him to push in harder but instead I find myself pulled into his arms and I'm filled balls deep.

"Fuck, Sugar. Your fucking mouth, you have no idea what you do to me." He grunts and pushes deep inside me.

I throw my head back, loving the feeling of fullness.

"Fuck, your pussy feels so good wrapped around my cock."

His words set my body alight and I tense up. "Right there," I scream out as I topple over the edge.

"Fuck, you're mine, Sugar. You'll always be mine."

He grunts with each thrust, leans forward and runs his tongue up my neck before biting down on my ear. It should scare the shit out of me after all I've been through but he ignites me and I come hard again.

"Yours, always yours, Knuckles." I kiss him deeply as I feel his hot release shoot inside me.

***

Looking out the window, I watch the moon rising and sigh against Sergio's chest, his hands twist in my hair.

"Paulie DeMarko"

I freeze up at the mention of the name but relax when his fingers massage my scalp

"He's a nasty fuck."

I run my nails over his hand with Marcella tattooed across it and wait for him to go on, I know this has something to with her and the asshole DeMarko.

"I was eighteen when my sister, Marcella, was snatched off the street. She had only gone to the local Deli to pick up an order our grandmother had placed earlier that morning." He blows out a deep breath "She was only sixteen at the time. I was busy doing some odd job for my grandfather. He wasn't part of the mafia but he dealt with them on occasion which is how I met Dominic. He and his father used to visit my grandfather. My sister and I lived with my grandparents because our parents had died in a car accident. When Marcella went missing I went nuts trying to work out who took her and why. Turned out my grandfather owed the wrong people money and he couldn't pay. He paid it back by giving him Marcella and making it look like she'd just disappeared."

He sighs loudly, I feel tears well in my eyes. What happened to his sister was what had happened to me.

"It took me a year to find out where DeMarko had her but, by the time I got there it was too late. He'd beaten her so badly and destroyed her in other ways to the point she was no good to him anymore. He pulled his gun and shot her in the head while I was forced to watch. Then, he turned the gun on me."

He takes my hand, places it on his chest and moves it over the scars.

"Dominic found me, saved my life and I stayed with him until I was back on my feet. Once I'd recovered, I went to my grandparents and told them what had happened. The look on their faces told me they didn't give a shit and they said I should thank my lucky stars I'd survived. They said Marcella's life had served its purpose by getting them out of trouble and now we could move on."

I gasp and cover my mouth as tears stream down my face.

"I was heartbroken over the way they thought of my sister as someone who could be thrown away. So, I shot them both and walked out of the house for the last time. When Dominic became boss, he accepted me into the family and I became a Grasso."

I'm silent, not sure what to say. He places his fingers under my chin, lifts my face to his and I see the sadness in his eyes. I want to kiss it away.

"DeMarko will *never* get his hands on you. I will set the world on fire to give you whatever you need and I will not have you taken away from me."

I kiss his soft lips and feel his hand on the back of my head but, before he deepens the kiss, there's something I need to tell him.

"I want you, Sergio. All of you. I didn't know what to think when I first saw you, I was so hurt, so scared. But, deep down I knew if I didn't let you in, I'd be missing something amazing. Even if it left me gasping for air, I was willing to let you fill the emptiness inside me. Whether that was for one fleeting moment or a lifetime."

"Mine," he growls while still holding the back of my head.

"Yours," I whisper back.

He takes my lips in a kiss which curls my toes. I crawl on top of him, feeling his hardness against my ass. I lift up to slide him inside when a knock sounds at the door followed by a little voice.

"Aunty Kirsty, mummy said it's time for dinner." I giggle at the sound of her sweet voice.

"Coming sweetie," I call back while never taking my eyes off my man.

He squeezes my ass. "I wish," he growls causing me to burst into laughter.

***

When I reach the kitchen, I look around and everyone who has become my family is gathered together and dinner is being laid out. Katherine is in Antonio's arms, I know I need to speak to her, tell her I'm sorry her father is dead even though I don't have a single regret about his death. I owe her that much, he was her father. When she looks my way, I indicate the back door, step away from Sergio's arms and head outside. The air is cool and I stand on the back porch breathing deeply. I have no idea how Katherine will respond to me, I want her to understand, I had to do it before he died.

When I hear her footsteps on the wooden deck I blurt out, "I'm sorry."

She comes to stand beside me. "For what, Doll?"

"Your father."

I watch as she looks up at the moon, her eyes are glassy and I wonder what she's thinking. Fuck, I hope she doesn't hate me.

"Please don't hate me," I whisper.

She turns to face me and I watch as her eyes soften.

"I don't hate you, Kirsty, and I'm certainly not upset he's dead. If anything, I'm relieved he can't hurt anyone else."

I nod, not sure what to say and she wraps her arms around me.

"He was a monster," I say into her shoulder

"Yes, he was and he deserved everything he got."

Easing back from the hug, I find she is smiling.

"He may have helped create me but he was no father to me. I'm not sure if you know the full story about what happened to me?"

I shake my head.

"Maybe one day I'll tell you. We all fight our own demons, Kirsty and I'm lucky enough to be surrounded by all these amazing people who help me through. Without them to build you up when you feel low, you become surrounded in darkness, not knowing what the light really means."

"Wow." I really soak in the words.

"Fuck, that was some deep and meaningful shit, wasn't it?" she laughs.

I nod and laugh with her.

"What I'm trying to say is, I've spent a lot of time pushing people and things away but I'm slowing learning to accept help. It doesn't mean you're weak, it makes you stronger."

I sob at her words, I understand exactly what she is saying.

"Kitten," Antonio calls out.

"Coming, Stud," she calls back which makes him growl and she laughs at him.

"Are you coming in for dinner?" Kat asks.

"I just need a moment, I'll be in shortly." She hugs me again before heading inside.

Taking a few steps into the back yard, I bend down, pick up a Dandelion and bring it to my lips. I know exactly what I want now. Closing my eyes, I let out a deep breath and blow. When I open my eyes, I watch as the puffs float around me before being lifted on the breeze into the night sky, taking my wish with them.

'I wish I may, I wish I might, for a love so strong the stars become jealous.'

Epilogue

One Month Later.....

Kirsty

I gaze at myself in the full-length mirror in the guest house at Brooklyn's home, knowing I need to get my butt into gear and go inside to give Brooklyn a hand to get into her dress. She warned last night it would be all hands on deck to get the thing on her, she even demanded Katherine bring a needle and thread to sew the bitch on her if she has to. No-one argued with her, with the way her hormones are right now, you never know what she might do. I like my life, actually I *love* my life so we just nodded. Kat and I shared a look when Dominic walked in and started telling her she was over reacting, for a mob boss he really isn't a smart man at all.

177

As for Sergio, he's amazing and still sexy as fuck to me. I doubt my opinion about that will change anytime soon. He finally confessed to me that the safe house we live in is actually his place. He said he hadn't had a use for it until I came along as it was easier for him to be at the guest house, close for when the Boss needed him. I didn't understand until he explained he was Dominic's personal bodyguard. I told him I was happy to stay at the guest house if that was what he preferred but, he reminded me how loud I am when we have sex and said he didn't want anyone hearing me. Sergio also liked being at his house because we could stay naked and he could have me anytime without someone walking in on us.

Turning my attention back to the image in the mirror, I can see how much I've changed in the past few months. My skin is clear with a healthy glow and according to Sergio, my eyes shine.

I feel his presence before I see him, when he enters the room, the energy changes and my body responds. Looking over my shoulder, I find him standing in the doorway studying me. He's wearing a suit which is molded to every part of his body, I lick my lips. Fuck he's sexy. I watch as his eyes take me in from head to toe and I have to squeeze my thighs together to prevent the ache which is building.

He crosses the distance between us in seconds and his mouth captures mine, I moan at the contact. When he pulls away, I watch as his eyes travel down my neck to my chest and a smile curves my lips. I shake my head, knowing exactly what it is that he'd prefer to be doing.

"Not this morning, Knuckles. I need to get my butt over to Brooklyn or would you prefer to deal with a very pregnant, hormonal, upset woman? I sure as shit don't want to upset her."

I laugh when his eyes widen and he shakes his head, my man isn't silly.

"Fanculo, Dominic digs a big enough hole every time he opens his mouth and I'm not joining him." He laughs and I turn back to the mirror to fix my lipstick.

Sergio reaches out and places a necklace around my neck and I gasp, it's absolutely stunning.

"Sergio...." I gasp again and run my fingers down the platinum chain to the crystal which hangs between my breasts. When I lift it, I see the delicate dandelion puff trapped inside. My eyes tear up, I turn and bury my face in Sergio's chest.

"Sugar, I love you." He kisses the top of my head.

Lifting my head, I grip his jacket in my fingers.

"Now, if there are no dandelions around to wish on, you only need to hold this in your hand."

He runs his fingertips down the side of my face and I shiver at the contact. Maybe we have time for a quickie after all? Standing on tiptoes, I brush my lips over his and tell him a secret I had intended to save for later.

"I love you, Sergio." I step back but stay focused on those midnight eyes which calm my soul. "I'm pregnant."

I watch and see the moment the words register; his eyes widen and his mouth slams down on mine. I moan and have every intention of stripping him out of his sexy suit when loud banging sounds at the door.

"Break it up, lovebirds. Kirsty, you are not fucking leaving me with Brooklyn. I love that woman but it's not happening so get your ass out here now."

I laugh at Kat and know I can't do it to her. After planting a kiss to Sergio's lips, I wriggle from his hold and head to the door.

"I'm the happiest man in the world, Sugar." I pause with my hand on the doorknob and smile over my shoulder.

"So am I, Knuckles."

I blow him a kiss and as I leave I hear him mutter, "wait until tonight."

My whole body ignites like a wildfire and I know the feeling will remain until I have Sergio buried deep inside me.

The End

for now anyways....

Trixie Mine

Trinity

I saw him.
One photo.
One look and I knew I was going to make him mine.
But the problem was, how do I make it happen?
All I have ever known are codes through a computer.
I've been kept hidden away, I only know what the world is like through a computer screen.
So, I guess I'll attract him to me the only way I know how.
With a swipe of a key and a click of the mouse, I'll lead him to right where I need him to be.
But, I have to be smart and not lead him straight to me because if anybody else finds out, especially my handler, I'm dead and so is he.
So, for now I'll keep picturing him in my dreams and hold onto the thought that one day, he will be mine.

Trixie: Theo will either catch onto my game and free me, or send me spiraling into darkness.

Theo

One coded message, that's all it took to start me chasing my tail.
A cat and mouse game which could be deadly.
But, then I saw her. Huge dark eyes surrounded by black framed glasses sucked the air from my lungs. How can one simple photo do so much?
A photo which seemed to take a lifetime to find.
But, there is one problem.
The only traces I can find of her is what she's feeding me through code to my computer. I need to find her now more than ever.
Someone has her.
They have taken what is mine.
But, they have underestimated me because nothing will stop me from getting her back.
Trixie is mine and I *will* find her.

Theo: I will chase her to the ends of the earth, and I will surrender to my knees for her to be mine.